"A Point In Time"

Book Two In the Dr. Ma Mystery Series

By Lenore Maio

I0550215

Dedication

To my family, friends, patients and clients who inspire me every day.

To my long suffering spouse for the time I take in my 'projects' I dedicate this book to you. If this book breaks into the hearts and minds of readers, we will celebrate.

To my Tech support guy, Barron Snyder, one of the finest men I have known. Thank you.

To all of you out there, wanting to write your story. Having the courage and vision to 'see' is simple. Taking the time to 'say' is more complex. Translating any story to a Universal language is well, a work in progress.

Thank you.

Introduction....from Dr. Ma

"So, how do you get a job like mine? I don't remember ever applying, or growing up thinking, "This, is what I am going to do."

"Actually, I don't remember ever growing up. Because I didn't. Grow up that is. I remember being an Elemental Spirit. Created from the element Air."

"I was formed into being for a purpose. My job. By a powerful Adept. What is an Adept exactly? That *is* a big question for sure. The title Adept, applies to those proficient in some form of, what humans would call, magic."

Is changing form, magic? Moving objects? Reading minds? Changing minds? Changing time? Making something like me?

There are doubtless hundreds of names for the individual who created this existence I have. I knew him, but I will call him Adept, only.

He did a good job with me, my mate, who is no longer, but was an Elemental tiger, and the replacement for my mate, David.

My name is Dr. Ma. I am an Elemental Air dragon. David, is an Elemental Earth tiger.

We both appear in human guise on the earthly plane of existence. At this moment, that is.

All three of us turned out pretty damn awesome. In fact, our Adept did a great job. I have accomplished amazing things to help humans in my time. I am not even tired of being here after 2,000 years, helping humans. I existed in my Elemental state, before becoming a dragon, far longer.

I would like a bit more change. Don't get me wrong. I am talking about the repetition of catching non human killers. That's the job.

There are never the same people, when I come back. Not too bad, if you don't become attached to anyone from the last time. I will miss Winnie, my clinic manager and assistant from this life, when it is time to go. Winnie and I have become close. As close as something of my nature can become.

I'll also miss Jeremy, my detective friend. Jeremy Brenner, is a talented young man and fun to work with. He is the Palm Beach cop who helps us with the murder cases. Or, do we help him?

David, my constant companion, will be coming with me. We both go together when we go. I was paired with him a thousand years ago. I miss him briefly, when he re-manifests in a human manner, by birth. Some strange, earth element requirement, birth.

Long ago for you, but not me, Buddha said something to the effect that the pain humans suffer was primarily from attachment. As a non human, living out a human existence to do my job, I can attest to that.

By the way, don't bother to correct me on quotes about Buddha or anyone from the past. I was there. I have always been there it seems. So unless you were there too, hush. Things change through the millennia in translation. You will most likely be wrong.

I know some brilliant minds, that cannot remember what was in their last meal, what composed yesterday's activity, nor are they able to access long term information, like a special day in their life correctly. Their mind is crowded with formulas, equations and ideas for world peace. Or World dominion.

Try it for over two thousand years or more. Wade through that many memories and thoughts to recall if it was a bagel or a danish with coffee that you had this morning.

Every day, I am inundated with human surety, that God, Buddha, Yaweh or whomever, *said exactly this or that* and *meant exactly this or that.* Those guys barely remembered what *they* had for breakfast. Trust me. They had more important thoughts crowding their heads.

Here is what is certain. You will be back when you die. Maybe not as aware as I am. So, remember that you have pre-planned what you will experience and learn each time around. I say, make a good job of it while you are here! Surprise yourself with your success. Or not.

Prologue

She stood over him, laughing, raising her arms overhead in triumph. Throwing her head back, she cried "Human fools!" Looking down at the apparently inanimate body lying crumbled at her feet, she pointed her long index finger and said, "Rise," in her commanding voice.

The man at her feet opened his eyes, and looked around startled, as if being woken suddenly from a nap. He scrambled to his feet and looked at her in surprise. "What happened," he began.

"Silence," she commanded. He felt his tongue freeze to the roof of his mouth. She held up something clutched in her left hand. He wasn't sure what it was at first. It appeared amorphous. Then it called to him.

"My soul!" He tried to scream around his frozen tongue. Nothing came out.

"Yes," she smiled. "You offered it did you not?"

He had of course offered his soul, his life, whatever, to collaborate with her, to have power on earth. To rule. Too late he was realizing, that after years of preparation, she had indeed come to him. She had asked what he was willing to give to her. Too late he was realizing, how he had answered. He had only told her what he would give, not what he wanted in return.

He remembered a flash of light and then darkness. Only darkness. No light of his soul rising from his body in death. He had remained aware. He thought he had died, that she had killed him for his trouble in calling to her.

"You will do something for me," she went on, ignoring his apparent distress. "When you are done, you will die." She started to turn away, then looked back at him. "Oh, and thank you for your service to me. Obviously you will not be rewarded with a long life. If that is what you had in mind." She walked away, chuckling to herself.

The further away she went, the more his being, his thoughts, faded from awareness. Soon, only his body stood there, looking out over the small marina. He turned and walked into the boat's control room and picked up the ringing phone.

"Hello," said Joseph McCarthy on the other end of the telephone line. "Are we ready to go?"

"Yes," replied the man, McCarthy's boat captain. At least that is what he still appeared to be. The man's soul had left with the Sorceress.

Table of Contents

Chapter One - In the Aftermath

Chapter Two - In the Library

Chapter Three - Joseph Goes Missing

Chapter Four - Tam and Dr. Ma

Chapter Five - Homecoming

Chapter Six - All In A Day's Work

Chapter Seven - The Case Unfolds

Chapter Eight - Jeremy and Gracie

Chapter Nine - The Murders in Review

Chapter Ten - A Trip to the Morgue

Chapter Eleven - To Kill a Tiger

Chapter Twelve - Resurrection

Chapter Thirteen - Circe and the Cetus

Chapter Fourteen - Finding Joseph

Chapter Fifteen - The Library

Chapter One - In the Aftermath

Main Guest Lodge, Luohu Tiger Reserve, South
Africa………

Soft lips swept over her collarbone leaving
chills in their wake. His arms wrapped around
her gently holding her, but with unmistakable
power. She felt his hands on her back through
the thin cloth of her shirt.

She knew, from those hands touching her
elsewhere, that they were hard and calloused,
but strangely smooth, no roughness to the
callouses.

She shivered again, feeling an odd sense of
fear mingle with the sexual excitement that had
raised the hairs along her skin wherever his
hands and lips had passed.

She opened her eyes as the fear grew more
persistent. Gorgeous tanned skin over rippling
back muscle and tousled blond hair greeted her
gaze. His lips travelled down past her
collarbone and continued south along her body.

He was stunning. She had seen him often this
past season, at events around Palm Beach. Tall
and imposing, with deep blue eyes and graceful

movements, he was the desire of many of the women and the men she knew. David was his name, an orphan of a wealthy family and a generous philanthropist in his own right.

Her father told her, that he had lived next to her parents, in the north end of Palm Beach Island, until he was about nine or ten years old. Both his parents had died suddenly, and he moved away, but that was all she knew. He remained an enigma to most.

"Karen," she had introduced herself, finally bold enough, or desperate enough to get to know him. They had talked forever it seemed, about her travels through the African continent, helping big game animal conservation efforts.

She knew one of his patients who also travelled to Africa for conservation. David was a local Acupuncture physician in Palm Beach County. She had been to the office he shared with Dr. Ma, another Palm Beach area philanthropist and David's business partner.

She knew they had a busy medical practice, and both taught in an attached martial arts school they co-owned. David didn't live off his substantial wealth, like so many kids she grew up with.

She and he had tried a couple of botched dates and she thought that was it. Until her father had asked David to come with her to South Africa. To protect her on her trip to a tiger reserve. There had been some recent violence in the area against tourists. "As a favor," her father told her about asking David to go.

She couldn't believe this was finally happening. That was all she had thought of, sex with him, even when he wouldn't talk to her before the trip. It had been her fault he wasn't talking to her. She had made some pretty big mistakes.

In Africa, so far from home, she was finally in his arms. His raw animal power was pressed against her, reminding her of what she witnessed. Was it yesterday? Had things happened so fast? Her brain was not working right. Trauma had fried some wires.

Trauma from the attack. The nighttime calm of their camp shattered by gunfire, screaming, and the smell of blood and fear. They had just gone out for an overnight game drive and bush sleep out with several porters and some armed security guards.

She had been standing, rooted to the spot in front of her tent, when she saw David run in to the center of the melee. He had looked at her briefly and turned away. Jumping towards the military style truck that had been regurgitating men with guns, she thought she saw him become a very large tiger.

"No, that could not be right!" She was still in shock. Nobody can turn into a tiger. She definitely, *did-not-see-***that***. She did not see a massive tiger, steel grey with black stripes actually. "No!" she told herself. There must have been a real tiger in camp. "But what tiger was that color, that size?"

Piles of bodies had been strewn around the camp, after the tiger attacked the men with guns. She had no memory of it attacking. It was as if her mind had gone completely blank to the devastation. But the bodies were real. Most were torn to shreds, guns useless at their sides. "Had she seen that *in detail*?"

Now, the two of them were back here at the Game Reserve lodge in her room. She clearly remembered being carried away from the camp. Fast. "But they had been almost 50 miles away from the Reserve main houses," she thought, her mind straying dangerously into crazy territory. "Someone was carrying her and running," she recalled. "Who? David?"

He pressed against her again as he picked her up off the floor, her legs wrapped around his waist. She had dreamed of being with him. The two of them where about to, what? Her mind was pulled back to the gruesome scene at the camp.

Questions pounded against the cage bars in her head where she was trying to lock away her memories. For safety. "How had she gotten here? Were all her men from the camp here? How many were among the dead?" she asked herself. She had only heard about a few porters coming back.

David kissed her mouth slowly. Her body turned to liquid in his arms. Warm liquid, spilling down over his body, and melting them together. It didn't matter what had happened, did it? All that mattered was right now.

Bam! Bam! Bam! Came the hurried pounding on the door before it suddenly opened. David dropped her on the bed, turning rapidly towards the noise. She scrambled backwards towards the headboard, panic rising easily. She was edgy from the insane events of the past, was it 24 hours?

She heard a strange sound and realized that David was crouched slightly between her and who was approaching from the living quarters of their suite. "Is he growling?" she thought, heart pounding. "No!" Stop the crazy thoughts about him turning into a tiger at the campsite," she chastised herself. Too much had happened there. Her mind had obviously fractured from stress.

The surviving porters she knew of, had arrived back at the lodge on foot. She had heard them tell the Reserve management, that they had seen a large tiger at a distance attacking the men with the guns.

The frightened porters had fled into the night when the shooting began. Her guards at the campsite had fired back at the interlopers. Violent men in the military style trucks had fired back at the guards, cutting her protectors down where they stood.

"The rumors were true about tourist murders," she had thought, terrified. "The men with guns would rob and kill them for what little they had."

The surviving porters, had hidden in the surrounding brush from the killers. From that vantage point, they reported seeing David running, carrying her away. Running in the direction of the main lodge of the tiger reserve.

Now, Karen looked up as a native born African porter came into view from the suite's anteroom. He looked harried and apologetic. The Luohu Tiger Reserve's guests were treated with respect and privacy, usually. When a mass killing and extreme violence hadn't wrecked the normal peace of the beautiful setting.

Hard on the man's heels, followed a short, stocky, white man. He was dressed in a meticulously tailored, three piece suit and tie. "Was she seeing things?" she thought. Karen stared, her mouth gaping slightly. "Who dressed like that in South Africa? At a wildlife reserve?"

David, who seemed to catch himself just before launching an attack on the poor porter, relaxed visibly at the sight of the white man in the meticulously tailored suit.

"Allistair!" he greeted him. "**What** are you doing here?"

"No time, David," Allistair replied in a clipped and efficient tone. "We have to leave. **Now**." He looked over at Karen cowering on the bed. "**Now**," he re-emphasized.

Karen noticed the porter was hurriedly shoving her things into open suitcases on the floor. She hadn't even noticed him pulling them out of the closet and armoire.

"Good morning," Allistair greeted her, offering a somewhat mirthless smile. "I am Allistair McGowan, David and Dr. Ma's solicitor. Please come with me immediately."

Karen apparently didn't move fast enough for Allistair. He nodded at David and said, "They're coming."

David bent over her on the bed, and swept her up into his arms. He rushed out of the room with her, following Allistair. Exiting the front entrance of the Reserve's guest lodge, Karen noticed the owners watching the whole scene nervously. There was a large black SUV with black tinted windows waiting in the front drive.

"It's okay, Karen," David said in a low, soft tone. "We are leaving before the authorities get here to avoid a political, and or legal mess. I am going to get you home to your parents in one piece as promised."

Everyone piled into the SUV. There were highly armed men in BDU's with rifles already in the driver and front passenger seats. Too frightened to say anything, Karen stayed silent.

David held her in his lap the entire wild ride to the apparently private airport. He still carried her, when they got out and rushed over to a large jet sitting on the runway.

"Where is this place?" Karen thought. This trip was full of surprises. She didn't know there was a private air strip so close. Especially something with a runway long enough for a jet.

A jet capable of international travel. A jet with no commercial airline's name on the side.

"Your belongings will follow by regular air travel, Miss," Allistair paused for her to offer her name.

"Karen," she almost whispered, in response.

"Karen it is then," he said, again offering her that mirthless smile. David placed her gently in a seat on the plush, private plane. "We have every amenity you will need while we are in flight," Allistair reassured her. "I even took the liberty of bringing you both a change of clothing."

David looked at Allistair surprised, his eyebrows raised. "Dr. Ma sent two changes of clothing ahead to the jet before takeoff," Allistair explained.

The interior of the plane was a plush and elegant version of an Emirates flight offering. Karen was on one going to Dubai last year with her father, for business.

Perfectly appointed private sleeping quarters, a central space with a bar, television for all on board, and an elegant dining menu were apparently also available for private jets if you had the money.

She had grown up with money, but this was a new one on her. "If Allistair was David's solicitor, how much money did David have at his disposal?" She looked over at him.

"David?" Karen asked in something louder than a whisper. She was finally finding her voice again, after Allistair's interruption of their almost lovemaking at the Reserve's Guest Lodge. "I think, I would like to lie down."

The jet had taken off shortly after they got on, and was cruising at an acceptable altitude. The male steward had told them they could walk around, several minutes ago.

David got up and lifted her to her feet. Arm around her, he supported her unsteady walk to a private sleeping suite. Helping her sit on the bed, he reached for a bottle of water and handed it to her.

He knelt on the floor in front of her. There wasn't enough room for him to sit next to her on the tiny bed.

"Drink this," he said, still speaking softly, soothingly. "You're going to get dehydrated if you don't drink enough, and I need to return you in good health."

Karen opened the bottled, surprising herself at how thirsty she was. She downed the contents in a few gulps. "What happened, David?" she asked. "Is everything going to be okay?"

David took her hands in his and bent his head over them. She thought it felt like he was blowing warm air between her palms.

Sleepiness overtook her suddenly. She felt him lie her down on the elegant bedding. Very softly she thought she heard him say, "Of course it will, sleep now."

David returned to the central cabin area and joined Allistair. "Drink?" his friend and lifetime legal counsel asked him, smiling grimly.

"If there ever was going to be a time this may be it," David said sinking into one of the deeply tufted leather chairs. "I am sticking to water, of course. I hope you are stocked with food?"

Allistair nodded at the steward rolling in a table, laden with the tiger's preferred fare of raw vegetables, fruits, nuts and seeds. A plate with a very raw steak and a glass of wine accompanied the array of food meant for David. This sparse plate would sustain Allistair's needs.

Elemental water snake that he was, he ate small amounts of food in human guise for show only. His real meals were taken in transitioned form, once a month, and they were large.

"How many did you kill?" Allistair said, around his first bite of steak. He was always one to get straight to the point.

David stopped wolfing down his food and looked at him. The pain of what happened was still raw on his face. "I, I'm not sure really," he said hesitating.

"They started shooting into the camp and I just attacked them. I don't even remember transitioning. You know I can't think clearly when there is blood everywhere in a fight like that."

Allistair chewed thoughtfully. "Doesn't matter," he said. I have people on the ground wiping the situation as clean as possible. The Reserve will get a substantial reimbursement for real and imagined losses.

The local police will get assistance, that may include new housing and educational funds for their children, and nobody will miss the bad guys."

"I think the writeup in the news," Allistair continued, swallowing a chunk of raw meat, and taking a large sip of Cabernet, "will be that the local police tracked poachers, turned roaming opportunist criminals against tourists.

They worked together with the Luohu Tiger Reserve's security force. All bad guys involved were killed in a gun battle on the Reserve's property. No animals were harmed. Peace was restored." Allistair finished speaking and sat back in his comfortable leather chair to sip his wine.

"Sounds like a win, win for the good guys," David said staring down at the remnants of the food he had all but inhaled. "I am going to take a shower and catch some downtime if it's okay with you."

The attorney watched him carefully a few minutes. "You put her out for the whole flight?" he said.

"No," David replied, "just a few hours. I need her to eat and hydrate."

"You want me to alter her memories?" Allistair asked. It was one of his Elemental abilities. He was second only to the powerful skills in memory manipulation of Dr. Ma.

"No," David said, shaking his head. "Not yet. We don't know what she actually thinks happened out there. This trip was important to her Foundation. I don't want her to lose memory of her time here."

"Your choice," Allistair said, getting up to pour himself another glass of Cabernet from the round bar area in the center of the room.

"How did you know to come get me?" David asked. "Ma-sama?"

"Oh, I picked up the phone as she finished dialing," Allistair said, his head cocked and eyebrows lifted. "I nearly fell out of my, um, bed, from that primal scream of yours. You forget how intimately we are all connected. You weren't far enough away for me not to hear that."

"We all know you don't sleep in a bed," David teased him, smiling for the first time since the campsite episode.

"Smart-ass," Allistair returned.

David's smiled faded briefly. "She heard me too," he said, referring to Dr. Ma. "I sensed her come to me right after I transitioned. I'm sorry, I didn't mean to put either of you through that."

Allistair put his hand on David's arm. "Don't be ridiculous, you didn't start the fight David, you just ended it. Get some down time, my friend, you need it."

David rose slowly from the deep leather chair. Stripping his shirt off over his head, he walked towards his suite to shower and rest.

"Is that a bruise?" Allistair asked, frowning. He pointed to a darkening area the size of a fist on David's side.

David looked down, surprised. "Looks like it," he answered. "I can't imagine why it hasn't healed. Everything else did."
"What is everything else?" Allistair asked, still frowning and staring at the area.

"Gunshots and a few hunting crossbow arrows," David replied almost shyly. He was not one to brag about his supernatural abilities.

"You need to show that to Dr. Ma when we get back," Allistair said.

David nodded and started walking away. Then he looked back at Allistair. "Thank you," was all he said.

Hours later, Karen stirred in her suite. Hearing her with his highly attuned ears, David got up from his deep, delta state meditation. He knocked softly on the panel that separated her area from the plane's center walkway.

"Karen?" he said softly. "May I come in?" There was no real door, just an expectation of privacy in the sleeping quarters with a partial privacy panel.

"David?" Karen answered sleepily. "Yes, of course."

He slipped around the privacy panel and knelt down to talk to her face to face while she lay on the small bed. He was 6'5" after all. Kneeling, he would be closer to her height.

"How soon before we are home?" Karen asked.

"We are about halfway there," he replied. "Would you like something to eat?"

"Yes, I'm starving," she replied. "How long was I asleep?" She was rubbing her face and stretching, trying to wake her body up fully. She hated the jet lagged feeling of intercontinental travel, but she loved traveling too much to stop.

"About 8 hours," David answered her. "You needed a good rest."

"I needed something else, before we were so rudely interrupted," she smiled slyly at him, remembering what they were doing when

Allistair and the porter barged in. She seemed to be recovered from her recent scare. David flushed slightly at her comment.

He didn't know what he had been thinking when he woke up in the morning at the Reserve Lodge, her still held in his arms. They must have fallen asleep with him not wanting to let go of her.

He had to keep her safe and next to him was the safest place right now. Her back had been curved into him, the length of her body warm and touching him almost head to toe.

Pure male instinct kicked in, and when she rolled over feeling his response to her, it just escalated from there. She hadn't been afraid of him that time.

Her hands all over him had answered that question. He bit his lip to erase the image for now. He tasted blood. Okay, maybe he needed to bite a bit hard to get control of himself.

"We can talk about that when we get you back safely," he said. Then he smiled at her to let her know he was just as interested in continuing things as she seemed to be. "Just not on the plane," he thought. "Not until things settle down at home either."

She sat up on the small bed now, looking more alert. Her stomach grumbled audibly.

"Why don't you have a shower and change into what Allistair brought for you. Then you can meet me in the dining area," he said.

Karen slipped her shirt over her head, looking at him hungrily and said, "You could join me."

David laughed out loud at that comment. "Not in that tiny shower, I couldn't. Wait until you see what I am talking about. I barely got a halfway decent wash up in mine while you slept. See you soon." He was gone before she could object.

When Karen finally arrived in the dining area, the male steward was bringing in a variety of dishes. Raw veggies, fruit and nuts for David and a large bowl of pasta and marinara sauce for Karen.

There was some type of custard for dessert and Allistair had already opened a bottle of wine to share with her.

He handed her a glass of wine as she walked up to them. She was freshly showered and attired in a soft lounge set from Juicy Couture. The outfit announced the label name proudly across her firm bottom.

"Thank you. Allistair is it?" Karen said. David was impressed by her memory after the traumatic events she had witnessed.

"That didn't bode well for what she would remember about him," he thought. David shook his head in the negative when Karen lifted her glass at him, inquiring by her gesture if he was going to join them.
"David doesn't drink alcohol," Allistair said by way of explanation. "It brings out the animal in him," he smiled.

David shot Allistair a dark look as Karen smiled and turned to him. "Really," she said, her tone of voice betraying her intentions. "We will just have to see about *that* when we get home."

"There is not a CHANCE of that happening in your lifetime girl," David thought. "You have no idea what it's like if I lose control. It will be hard enough to be intimate with you without scaring you or scaring me really."

Outwardly, David smiled, and said nothing. He was going to swat that snake around like a toy for this. Allistair's smile faded somewhat as David's thoughts reached him.

"Let's have dinner," Allistair announced, taking Karen's arm gallantly for the two foot trip to her dining chair.

They still had many hours in the air before landing in the USA.

Chapter Two - Homecoming

David had plenty of time to contemplate the awful reality of what happened near the Luohu Valley Reserve on their plane trip home.

He remembered hearing Karen speak at various fundraisers for her Save the Tiger Foundation in Palm Beach. The particular reserve they were to visit was created in 2002 out of 17 defunct sheep farms. South China tigers were brought there for re-wilding before being returned to their native Asia.

The word luohu, from the name of the Reserve, meant tiger in Chinese.

The Luohu Valley Reserve was breeding re-wilded South China tigers (Panthera tigris amoyensis). By 2015, there were 20 wild tigers living in the protected area of the Reserve.

This is what they had gone to see. Karen eagerly told him when they arrived that those 20 tigers, represented about 20% of the world's population of that critically endangered subspecies.

David and Dr. Ma had given generous donations to her fund. It was a personal issue for David to help his own kind. Well, sort of his own kind. Dr. Ma had told him that she hoped he would donate for her, when and if, they found a Save the Dragon group. They both had laughed and she wished him well on the trip.

Allistair took care of all the particulars when Dr. Ma or David travelled. Meeting with David before he left, Allistair had frowned and pointed to several online articles detailing increasing violence against tourists in cities and outlying human populations near the Reserve.

"I don't like it," Allistair had told David in his carefully controlled tone. Poachers are getting braver and more likely to maim and kill tourists for money and possessions. The gang violence in the cities, especially Cape Town is out of control."

"We will be fine, Allistair," David tried to reassure him. "The Reserve has its own security force, and Karen said there have been no known incidents there. It is one of the largest protected areas in South Africa."

Allistair had merely frowned more deeply and shaken his head.

David was going as a promise to Karen's father, Joseph McCarthy. The man was getting up in years and felt he couldn't handle the rigors of the trip. Rumors about violence prompted him to enlist David's help.

The fact that David and Karen had an uneasy relationship from recent events was no deterrent to Joseph's request.

Uncomfortable, but feeling he couldn't refuse the older man, David agreed. He had no worries for himself regarding the violence in the area they were traveling to. Almost nothing existed on earth that could harm him personally. It was Karen he had to worry about.

The flight and arrival had gone smoothly. The Luohu Reserve was near Philippolis in the Free State section, part of it spanning the Orange River in the upper reaches of the Vanderkloof Dam in the Northern Cape.

He had been astonished at the beauty of the grasslands of the Valley. Lower-lying flat areas, dense stands of shrubs and trees next to rivers and Acacia karoo woodlands met his gaze from the main guesthouse.

The tigers were in an enclosed and protected section, but David and Karen were also here to see the wildcats, caracals, and black-backed jackals. A nice assortment of predators overall. Those animals were just further down the food chain predator pecking order from the tigers.

The low lying plains were dotted with a varied diet for a predator, zebras, crested guinea fowl, Egyptian geese and South African ostriches roamed freely.

David's deep Elemental earth tiger instinct wanted to be free to roam and revel in the beautiful landscape. He had to remind himself what his actual purpose had been in coming here with Karen.

They had taken the opportunity to set up a campsite in the actual Reserve for a night or two, with a staff of game wardens (armed guards really) and domestics (porters) who were familiar with the particular issues that arose camping in a wild life area.

The first night everything had fallen apart when the men with guns arrived.

How the men got in past security and perimeter fencing, who knew? How they had found the camp wasn't easily answered either. The thick brush where they were set up would have partly hidden them even from night vision used on the surrounding flatter plains. If local criminals like that could even afford night vision.

The trucks and weapons seemed of very good quality, but David was no expert on what bad guys in the area had available.

The painful memories overcame him as he lay in his private sleeping quarters on the jet. He remembered that the first day had passed uneventfully as they drove around, observing the animals. When night had taken over the campsite it was brightly lit, making the surrounding darkness even deeper in color.

The sound of the engines from the trucks as they approached was loud in the relative silence of the South African plains.

There was confusion among their perimeter guards, at first. Was someone coming from the main house on the Reserve? Had something happened? Then the shooting began, and it was too late to have any more thoughts, other than to survive.

After it was over, after there were no more shots fired, no more screams, he found himself transformed back to his human guise. The whole thing had passed in a blur of blood, teeth, and claws.

He was kneeling in the dust and dirt of the now ravaged campsite, bodies scattered around him in disarray. The limbs of the so recently dead had settled this way and that, some still holding their automatic weapons and machetes.

Not good enough to protect them from his vicious response to their attack. Not nearly enough to fight back against the massive physical power he displayed in his Elemental tiger form.

"But fair is fair, and they had started it hadn't they?" Charging into camp to kill, maim, steal and maybe kidnap the pretty white girl for sale as a slave on the black markets later.

Nonetheless, killing fragile humans tore at his non human soul. They had no chance to survive him. It was never a fair fight and it wasn't exactly what he was tasked with doing here, was it?

He had finally stopped his silent sobbing. The only evidence of his grief had been the shaking of his whole body and the tears running through the fingers splayed across his face.

Ma had heard him when all hell broke loose and he transformed. She sensed the cosmic shift of the event and had come to him. Not to mention the primal scream he always let loose before jumping into a fight.

Allistair had heard him a continent away. Others would have as well. Otherworldly ears only of course.

Ma had arrived in spirit. Nobody would see or sense her presence but him or another Otherworldly. David and Dr. Ma were bound closely. That is why she came. This bond kept them aware of each other's activity even if they were thousands of miles away as they were right now.

Her anger at him being in peril had been overwhelming as he felt her approach. She would have wanted to be there in real time. Even at her incredible flight speed, she did not possess the ability to spontaneously appear in full physical form.

"Yet," he thought. She never failed to surprise him with new skills as they travelled through time together.

David had opened his eyes to take in the full scene of bodies, blood and gore around him. He could imagine what it would have looked like if she had been there fighting with him.

The situation would not have needed them both. He would have simply grabbed Karen and run, taking her far from any view of the carnage.

Ma would have left a pile of small, charred human pieces. Not much more. She was cold and calculating. They would have been killed quickly and efficiently, pilled up, and set on fire.

Dragons like a clean field when they are done. No rotting stench to taint the air from which they were born.

Tigers, on the other hand, had no problem with scattering the soon to be rotting fertilizer of human body parts around. They could then enrich the earth where they were originally formed.

His head had jerked up instinctively when he heard a noise, his body following in a split second. He had heard sounds too faint for human ears.

Karen hadn't moved from her original location in her state of shocked incomprehension.

She still stood by the gaping tent opening. What was left of the tent. Her hand still clutched the shredded fabric that once formed a zipped closure.

"David! They are coming, go!" he heard Ma clearly in his mind, urging him to vacate, and fast.

"Yes," he thought. Engines, loud voices, still miles away but out here it left a clear line of approach to come after them unless they hurried. If you knew where you were going that is. Must be coming to see what their now past caring companions had accomplished. Not much. They had not expected him.

The scent of oil, gasoline and sweat drifted lightly on the air as David rose and closing the gap between them in one swift stride, picked up Karen and tossed her onto his back. He wrapped her hands around his neck and her legs around waist to stabilize her. She complied and hung on for dear life.

He had turned away from the smells and sounds and just ran. He had varied terrain around him but there was nowhere really to hide. Only distance to give them a semblance of safety. He didn't need to transform again to his tiger being. In human form, he was one of the fastest beings around on foot.

Karen made a small noise when he grabbed her initially but no further sound came as he sped away. He had headed instinctively towards the closest human outpost that would shelter them from the gang that had killed so many in their camp.

The beautiful and exclusive headquarters for the Reserve they had come to visit. An elegant, almost spa like oasis with armed guards to keep wealthy visitors safe while they decided on spending money to save endangered wildlife.

It was about 50 miles away from where he started. He ran in the direction of the then rising, early morning sun.

What he didn't know, was what had been happening between Dr. Ma and Allistair. Her presence had faded as he ran toward the Reserve's lodge.

She had only been there in spirit anyway. There was not much she could do in that form. That she had tried yet anyway.

There was plenty for her to do in her human guise back in the States.

At home in Palm Beach County, Florida, Dr. Ma tapped her foot impatiently as the phone rang longer than she felt was acceptable for a highly paid personal solicitor.

There had better not be an answering machine! In truth, Allistair answered in two rings.

She had been on her morning run when she heard David's guttural scream. It was a war cry really. All the Otherworldly beings around her had heard it too. She froze for a moment. The scream resounded through her human body like something tangible.

She was steps away from Jamil's tree. She had rushed towards him and pressed her body up against his gnarled and ancient exterior. Jamil's power would support and shield her while she joined David in ethereal form only. She had to see what was happening. Hopefully no passing humans would notice her hugging the tree.

Probably not. Jamil was powerful. She may just appear to be part of his tree for a little bit. To human eyes that was.

The sight that had greeted her on arrival told the story. David kneeling in the dirt, shoulders shaking silently as he cried. Anger tore through her. Anger overwhelmed her as she studied his surroundings. The sound of an approaching truck engine and voices spurred her to warn him. "Go," she had urged him.

A voice replaced the ringing in her ear. "Yes Ma-sama?" Allistair McGowan answered on his personal cell phone. "I heard him too," he added before she could begin speaking.

"Is that a slight hissing quality to your voice I hear, Allistair?" Dr. Ma had inquired. "It's 11:00 AM. You should have been up, fed and working for hours. Were you lingering over breakfast again?"

"I was still asleep," Allistair had responded, somewhat defensively. " I had a late night last night."

Dr. Ma did some quick calculations in her head. It was close to Allistair's monthly feeding time. That was why he was sleeping in today.

Allistair McGowan had been Dr. Ma's private solicitor since her first earthly plane manifestation. Like her, he simply replaced his human body when he needed to occupy a new existence. They would age to a certain point and jump ship to the body being sustained for that very purpose.

The Spirit animating the human body they took would have been born into it, and lived life up to the point of their 'moving in' so to say. That was their job, the Spirit's, to provide a new vessel for the Elemental to continue their endless existence.
It certainly simplified their business affairs.

In Allistair's case, he always produced an heir and that is who he became when he was ready. Only one heir. Since Elementals didn't reproduce with humans, his human wives always had to be artificially inseminated.

That was good for Allistair. He could make sure his features would be well represented in his offspring by choosing the right wife and right egg donor.

In times past, he would chose a man who looked like him and then kill and eat him when his wife was pregnant. A bit of memory manipulation would ensure his wife thought it was him having sex with her, not a substitute.

Soon enough he would be able to just clone himself in a new embryo. He was excited by the possibility!

The massive green Anaconda that he became in transition to his Elemental water snake, was an impressive sight. That was something his human wives never saw of course. If that ever happened, Allistair would employ the same memory manipulation.

The wives would never see him transitioned, nor any other human that would live to tell the tale. Allistair did not have the same sensibility as David and Dr. Ma when it came to not killing humans.

He wouldn't go out of his way to harm them. Not at all. He may dispose of someone who saw him transform and could leak his secret to the world. "A large meal is a large meal," he would say to Dr. Ma when the topic was broached. Ma always cringed at the thought. She killed, not ate her foes.

Dr. Ma had known Allistair for two thousand years. Give or take a century here and there. David met him a millennia later, when he was joined with Dr. Ma. Joined after her first tiger mate had left this plane of existence.

David had not come to her as another mate. Dragons usually mate for life. He was manifested to help her with her job of protecting humans from otherworldly killers.

He would be the balance of Yang energy for her Yin energy. Dragons and tigers, had been trapped in that endless cycle of embrace and attack, as a yin and yang balance, according to Chinese mythology since time began. Whenever that was.

"I need you to take the jet," Dr. Ma began.

"And go get David and his little girlfriend in South Africa," Allistair finished for her. "Yes, I heard that bone chilling primal scream he does when he starts fighting from here. I'm sure every Otherworldly between Miami and South Africa heard it too. Nearly gave me a heart attack."

Dr. Ma chuckled, even though she was not in an amused mood at all right now. "You should hear it in person, standing next to him. It would freeze your pee mid stream, snake man," Ma laughed.

"Oh, something to look forward to," Allistair replied. "I have the jet ready at the airport, flight plan paid for in advance, no questions. I will take off as soon as I can get there."

Anaconda are slow movers out of water. Allistair moved almost as slowly, physically, in human guise as he did when a snake. His mind however was agile, with a super fast processor.

"Shake a leg, Allistair," Dr. Ma admonished. "If something happens to David before you get there," she didn't finish the thought. She was a bit overprotective of him. The tiger would be fine if he were alone. She was worried he would let something happen to him to protect the young woman he was with.

"In the big scheme of things, she is expendable," Allistair said, seeming to read her thoughts. "Shake a leg? Getting personal I see."

"He will never let that happen," Ma almost snapped at him, referring to Karen being expendable. "I am just trying to get you going. Why did I let him go solo, Allistair?" she said. "He is too young."

Allistair laughed, " That has to be a first, a thousand year old Elemental being considered, *too young*."

"You had better be at the airport by now," Ma said. Her tone had changed considerably. The strange quality of her timbre indicated she was closer to dragon than human. Anger and fear does that to Elementals. They revert to true form.

"I've got it," Allistair sighed. "I have people on the ground mopping up as we speak. Nobody will get to him before I do."

"It's a 16 hour flight," Ma said, still fighting her anxiety over David's well being.

"Everything will be fine," Allistair had said, changing to a conciliatory tone. Dr. Ma thought it was a bit hissy for her taste.

"You had better be right," was the last thing she said before hanging up.

Allistair did not misunderstand the threat in her tone. The great dragon would pick him up and drop him back to earth from a height high enough to freeze him solid if he didn't fix things asap. It wouldn't kill him in his Elemental form but, it would hurt like hell.

He was shouting to his driver as he ran down the hall in his sumptuous Miami mansion. His human service staff was used to his odd hours and even odder demands.

Everyone was up and scurrying around to get him out the door and en-route to the airport in record time.

Taking care of the needs of otherworldly beings around the globe had its idiosyncrasies for sure. Especially regarding Dr. Ma and David.

Dr. Ma hung up the phone and turned to her computer screen. An email from Detective Jeremy Brenner was displayed. Just what she needed, more drama.

Apparently Karen's father, Joseph, was missing. Dr. Ma had not shared this piece of information with Allistair. He had only one thing to be concerned about in her estimation, David.

It was her day off. She replied to Jeremy's email that she would meet him for lunch at Pizza Al Fresco in Palm Beach. It was right next to David's apartment. She had been checking on his stunning orchid collection while he was away. She would go there first.

Beautiful Vanda orchids hung in his floor length second floor apartment windows. They always seemed to be in bloom, with the care he gave them. Purples, yellows, pinks and green flowers covered the main stems with long leaves spiking out of the sides and tangles of roots below.

The tiger was an enigma even to her. His extreme capability for violence blended harmoniously with the care of delicate flowers and a gentle, genial nature.

They had been together a thousand years now she and he. Working side by side to protect humans from Otherworldly killers as she and her mate had done for a thousand years before. David was his replacement. Another tiger to balance her dragon and keep things running smoothly.

They were not intimate she and David. He had never had a mate in his time here. He couldn't really have a true mate, could he? Only if she were his mate.

Sexual partners he could have for the asking. The absolutely gorgeous young man was never at a loss for someone wanting to get to know him better. A lot better.

But dragons mate for life, and she already had had her mate. He then passed from this plane of existence and left her behind. She too could have any manner of human companionship like David, but it was never the same.

Neither could interact with Otherworldly creatures in an intimate manner. Well, not without consequences. The balance of power would slide sideways.

Unless they were off this plane of existence.

She could leave this plane, but David couldn't. She tried to never leave him on the earthly plane long, like when she went to seek information from the library that Allistair and she kept on an alternate plane of existence.

The real Library of Alexandria.

Hell, look what happened when she simply let David go to South Africa for a fundraising trip with Karen? She parked her Mercedes C63 AMG Coupe on Peruvian and paid the parking meter for a few hours. She didn't know how long this would take.

Running lightly up the stone stairs to David's sanctuary, she fished his door key out of her small Hermes handbag.

Even for a casual lunch, Dr. Ma was dressed fashionably in Lafayette NY 148 linen pants and one of their crisp cotton blouses. Her ever present Louboutin heels completed the look. Long straight black hair fell to her waist.

Dr. Ma loved fashion when she wasn't in martial arts gear, workout clothes or a lab coat. Today, she wrapped a multicolored pearl necklace from Simon Sebbag around her elegant neck and placed a thick wavy silver cuff from the same designer on her wrist.

Tall, lean and muscular from years of daily training and a stellar diet had shaped Ma's figure into something any fashion or style would look great on. At 55 years of human age, she was beautiful and the envy of the women who knew her for her untouched beauty.

David's door key was just for human observation. Dr. Ma placed her fingers gently on the hidden security rune next to the door jamb to actually gain entrance.

She had this type of security at her home as well. Human burglars or unwanted human solicitors would never know exactly why they didn't want to enter his apartment, or her home for that matter. They would just suddenly decide that they didn't and leave.

The security rune kept out Otherworldly creatures too. Neither Dr. Ma nor David wanted to come home to any surprises.

A calm and peaceful ambiance greeted her. The orchids were rustling in their sensual plant speech, anticipating her misting their roots with David's special mixture. The 100 year old stone walls held some rare artifacts from around the world and the highly polished wood floor gleamed as if it had never been walked on. Like Dr. Ma, David had an Otherworldly housekeeper.

They both employed djinn from their ancient homelands. One djinn would keep everything in perfect order. Hers had, for 2,000 years in her employ.

David's was somewhat forgetful at times. The creature was ancient, older than Dr. Ma even. Despite Ma's suggestions, David wouldn't send her away. Even with her less than stellar work. She could have lived anywhere in peace and oblivion but the djinn, a tiny female of mixed origins, wanted to stay with him as well.

Ma wasn't quite sure where David had found her, but she was loyal to him and he to her. Didn't keep the ancient djinn from almost burning down his last apartment trying to cook something. This was why Dr. Ma checked in daily. Nothing to worry about then.

Locking up after she was done with the orchids, she smiled to herself. She had found the djinn sleeping soundly and left her that way. Dr. Ma walked the 100 feet through the via by Renato's Restaurant to their casual lunch venue, Pizza Al Fresco.

Detective Brenner was sitting at a table waiting for her. Next to him sat a too thin and once quite lovely woman in designer attire. She had that typical, stretched too tight, aloof air of so many older female Palm Beach residents. Ann McCarthy, Dr. Ma assumed from Brenner's email topic. She would apparently be part of their lunch discussion.

Dr. Ma extended her hand as she sat down. "Dr. Ma," she introduced herself to Ann McCarthy.

Ann took Ma's hand delicately in her fingers and said, "Ann McCarthy."

Dr. Ma noted the hollows under her eyes. She must really care about her husband being missing. Not always the arrangement here on the island of Palm Beach," Ma thought.

"So, Detective Brenner," she addressed him formally, " What can I do for you and Mrs. McCarthy?"

Chapter Three - Joseph Goes Missing

"My husband has gone missing Dr. Ma," Ann McCarthy said. "He went out on his boat with our Captain two days ago and hasn't been seen or heard from since."

Detective Brenner waited for Ann to pause and give him the opportunity to speak. "Of course we have all the usual agencies and so forth on notice and looking for him."

Ann McCarthy interrupted with, "Yes, you are doing the best job you can I'm sure. I understand you have consulted with the police before Dr. Ma, and are something of a psychic. I believe in psychics. I want to hire you to find Joseph for me."

There was a slight waver in her speech when she said her husband's name. Dr. Ma noticed Jeremy Brenner picked up on it as well. Moist eyes in the practiced self composure of a life long socialite and a voice tremor? Good as a polygraph result. She was upset and fearful regarding her husbands whereabouts.

"I am not exactly a psychic Ann, but I do help the police. There is no need to hire me. I will help Detective Brenner find your husband," Dr. Ma said slowly, watching Ann McCarthy's reaction.

The other woman visibly relaxed. Dr. Ma had that effect. Her voice seemed monotone, but was often quite hypnotic. She wanted to put the distraught woman at ease. "Your daughter and my colleague, David Anderson, should be landing in Miami soon. Did you know they were on their way back?"

"No I didn't know that they were back so soon," Ann McCarthy said with a slight frown. "I thought they would be a few more days. Miami did you say? I thought they were going through New York."

"They had to cut their trip short due to some local goings on, so they took a private charter back," Dr. Ma explained, still watching Ann for her reactions. All she saw was mild confusion. The mother and daughter were obviously not close.

Ann's eyes narrowed slightly. "Hmph," she said. "I assume she will want her father to pay for that expense, instead of her Foundation. He gives her anything she wants, always has."

"Yep," Dr. Ma thought. Not close that mother and daughter. Aloud she said "Not a concern, my solicitor used our company jet to pick them up. We will write it off as another donation to the Save the Tiger Foundation. My colleague has already given to them generously."

Detective Brenner sat in silence, munching on the bread the waiter had now refilled, twice. He was ready to order lunch, but a good detective never stops a conversation that may be of evidentiary value. Or, just plain interesting.

"David," Ann suddenly focused on Dr. Ma as if seeing her for the first time. "Oh, you and David are the philanthropists Karen discussed."

Ann McCarthy handed her menu to the waiter standing by her patiently. "Mixed greens salad with lemon juice." It wasn't on the menu, but the denizens of the island could ask for anything short of an endangered species on their plate, and get it.

Detective Brenner said, "The usual," and Dr. Ma echoed his comments. They ate there frequently enough for the staff to know their preference. Brenner would have a large bowl of the house pasta fagioli soup and a large bowl of fettuccine Alfredo. Dr. Ma preferred the lentil soup. She was not a big eater at lunch, or anytime really.

Ann McCarthy was looking between Dr. Ma and Detective Brenner as if trying to remember something. "Oh!" she said again, suddenly. "David lived next door with his parents who were killed when Karen was at boarding school. I think she brought him home a couple times recently to, what do they call it today, *hook up.*"

Detective Brenner coughed, barely saving himself from splitting soup on Ann McCarthy with a quick grab of his napkin. She just looked up at him, oddly. "I will have to find out what that is all about," Dr. Ma thought to herself.

Jeremy wouldn't meet Ma's gaze and Ann McCarthy continued talking.

"My husband asked him to go with Karen to protect her." The woman's eyes drooped, exhaustion was fighting with her practiced social expression. "I wish he had gone with Joseph, to protect *him.*"

Detective Brenner had worked his way through his soup. He stopped eating to give Dr. Ma more background, still not looking directly at her. "No sign of Joseph's boat has been found,

Dr. Ma. Its as if they went out of the Jupiter harbor and disappeared. No boaters, vessels or even radar picked them up after they were last seen. All the equipment on his boat was in working order and there has been no communication from them."

Dr. Ma digested this information as she slowly spooned the delicious lentil soup into her mouth. Always the consummate physician, she believed a proper digestion came from eating in peace.

When she finished her bowl she said, "Ann, you haven't touched your salad, can we have them get you something else?"

Ann McCarthy looked up surprised. She didn't realize she had been sipping her wine without a bite of food. "No," she said. "I am not particularly hungry." She suddenly stood up. "I must get back to the house in case Joseph calls. Thank you for assisting the police Dr. Ma."

Then she walked away, Chanel handbag tucked carefully under her arm. Her posture was stiff and upright in her perfectly fitted Chanel suit and heels.

"Poor thing," Dr. Ma observed to Jeremy Brenner. "She is a wreck. I wish she and Karen were closer since her daughter will be home by tomorrow, but, let's get on with it. What haven't you told me so far?"

He looked at her and raised his eyebrows in surprise. "Nothing actually. We have absolutely nothing to go on at this moment."

Dr. Ma paused to think. "I will need the exact coordinates Joseph's boat was last seen and any information on where he was going that day."

"I have it right here," Jeremy replied. He tore off a small sheet of notepaper from his ever present old fashioned pocket pad and gave it to her.

Dr. Ma smiled. "Are you going to go more high tech one day my friend?" she said. "Also, what was with the reaction when Ann mentioned David and Karen hooking up?"

"Never will I go more high tech," he replied grinning. His smile faltered slightly and he said, "Karen and I dated briefly, but it is long over." He got up to leave. "I have to get back to the office. Mrs. McCarthy took care of lunch by the way."

Dr. Ma nodded. "I will have to thank her sometime," she replied.

Watching Jeremy walk away, Dr. Ma pulled out her cell phone to check for messages from Allistair. So far, they were en-route safely in the jet. Nothing had occurred to delay them at the lodge or the airport. All bodies and payoffs had been taken care of. Neither Karen nor David was the worse for wear.

Dr. Ma was relieved. One less concern. David would be fine now. Allistair and he were a formidable pair. She would see him soon and he could help her with the latest mystery, Joseph's disappearance.

She also needed him to get back to work. Handling all their patients and classes at the dojo for the days he had been gone was a bit much.

Winnie was grumpy about the backup in his absence. Dr. Ma thought Winnie just missed him. "Me too, Winnie," she thought.

She headed towards Starbucks. A quick coffee pick me up and some shopping would clear her mind. She needed to do something completely non work related. Then she could concentrate on finding Joseph McCarthy.

"Where are you," she said softly to herself as she strolled down Worth Avenue. She didn't expect him to answer her. Not if he was still alive.

Hours later, she returned to her Mercedes. She had asked the maitre d' at Renato's to add to her parking meter in the event she was running late. No ticket. "Good job," she thought.

All her purchases would be delivered to her house in the next day or so. Only tourists lugged bags and packages they bought from the shops in Palm Beach.

Locals wouldn't want to inconvenience themselves lugging parcels about Town. At first, she drove towards home. Changing her mind, she turned her car towards her friend's bike shop in West Palm Beach.

She would ask Tam for help finding Joseph. The local bike shop owner was a human/ Otherworldly mix. Half Wind Spirit and half human, he chose to live in the human plane of existence on earth.

Dr. Ma knew it wasn't easy. Half bred children were extremely rare. Conception was not known to occur between Otherworldly beings and humans.

When it did, the stress of choosing between the two realities often drove the half bred creature a bit mad. In Tam's case, he drank alcohol to ease the discomfort. He also rode competitively and worked ceaselessly on projects to support local cyclist safety on the roads. His shop sponsored all kinds of events.

Tam had helped Dr. Ma and David with their last case, a murder of a young woman cyclist on Bingham Island off Southern Boulevard causeway in Palm Beach. She had known the Wind Child for many years. He was a reliable source of information for her.

"Dr. Ma!" Tam greeted her as she walked in the shop. Tam's shop was always overflowing with everything a cyclist could and possibly never knew they needed or wanted. Everything was neat and orderly, there was just a lot of it.

Tam employed a few bike mad folks in his shop. They had been in the same ratty location for 20 or 30 years now Ma figured. He said he couldn't afford better digs with what you made on selling and repairing bikes. Dr. Ma believed him.

They were alone for the moment in the shop. The smell of the shop's overworked cappuccino and espresso machine permeated the air.

"What was the tiger ripping to pieces this time?" Tam inquired with a sly smile. Like many Otherworldly beings, he had heard David's war cry. The one that Allistair had complained about so bitterly.

"That is a good question, Tam," Ma said carefully. "I understand some less than honorable individuals may have mistaken him for someone that was defenseless against their human weapons."

Tam chuckled softly and made a face that indicated he was sure they had not made the best decision. "Too bad, so sad," he said, working without pause on the bike he was repairing. "Got what they deserved I guess."

"Perhaps a bit more than that," Dr. Ma said, thinking about the pile of body parts and lake of blood. "Poor Karen," she thought to herself. "I wonder what she saw, or understood?" Ma was sure David would explain everything when he got home.

"Is he back yet?" Tam inquired. " Where was he? I could tell he wasn't close, but not exactly where he was."

"South Africa," Ma replied.

Tam looked at her, raising his eyebrows in surprise. "Wow," he said. "That cat is loud." Then he smiled as if realizing his play on words

Dr. Ma smiled back and then said, "I need your help again Wind Child."

Tam nodded his assent and she continued. "The woman David went to South Africa with, her father is missing off the Jupiter Inlet. He took his boat out and there is no sign of him, the boat or the Captain."

Tam continued to work on the bike repair but he nodded again to indicate she should continue.

"I want to go out there tonight and check the area he was last seen. David will be back tomorrow, but I don't want to wait. I may have already missed something. Would you be willing to come along?"

Tam paused, mulling it over. It was unlikely he would refuse the dragon's request. "I have the Wellington ride tonight and then I will meet you at your house if that works," he said

"Perfect," she replied.

The front door of the shop opened and one of Tam's mechanics came in bearing a big box of donuts, balanced on a large pizza box from a local chain. "Hungry, Dr. Ma?" the young woman said.

Dr. Ma laughed. "No, thank you. I just had lunch a half hour ago. I am always amazed at the crappy food you guys eat here." The young woman laughed back.

"Coffee?" she inquired of Dr. Ma. "Make you faster on the road."

"Somehow I have heard that before. No thank you," Ma said. She left the shop and headed home to get ready for tonight. A quick trip to the Library for research would be in order. She needed to know everything about the coordinates that Jeremy Brenner had given her.

The last place Joseph McCarthy and his boat Captain had been seen.

The South Florida day was basking in full sunlight as she drove east over the Okeechobee Boulevard overpass. I95 traffic was moving smoothly.

Palm trees lining the road and the glittering water catchment areas to her left and right made a Chamber of Commerce type of picture. Dr. Ma gave a silent thanks to the Universal design that blessed her path this time around.

"Two thousand human years, and I am not tired of my job yet," she thought as she headed towards Flagler Drive and home.

She had seen so many civilizations come and go and lost so many people she had come to care about in her many re-manifestations.

"Even my mate, the love of my life," she mused. She hoped that she wasn't destined to lose a tiger companion every thousand years. Other than Allistair and a few ancient Otherworldly creatures, she alone had been here the longest.

Arriving home, she took out her house key in case any human eyes were watching. Placing in the door lock for effect, she surreptitiously touched the security rune, allowing her to enter.

Her djinn housekeeper was flitting from room to room on what appeared to be a dust removal mission.

Her house was calm and quiet outside of the djinn's activity. She walked past the front entrance and through the center of the large airy home. She always felt at peace here. The security rune did its job.

Otherworldly beings would not be able to remain in the immediate vicinity without a specific invitation. Her Elemental magic protecting the home and grounds was strong. She had to deactivate much of it for her guest to be able to enter.

"Tam will be here later tonight," she silently told the magic that activated the rune. "You can rest now."

She would be home when Tam arrived this evening. No need for the system to be fully armed. She was much worse for any intruder than the system ever would be. If you weren't invited that is. Even if she wasn't here, there was her djinn. They were powerful.

"First things first," she told herself. "Visit the library."

Ma walked through her spacious living room and out onto the back patio. As she passed the fountain that was delicately splashing water into a large stone basin, she touched the female stone figure's shoulder.

"Hello Berenice," Ma greeted the librarian as the stone figure opened its distinctly almond shaped eyes. The iris of the eyes that were now lapis blue instead of stone. The same color as Dr. Ma, David, and all Otherworldly creatures. It was a definite 'tell' if you knew what you were looking for.

The stone was animated by the Spirit of a queen from the Ptolemaic reign in Egypt. She was instrumental in saving the majority of the content from the Library at Alexandria.

History books and writings recording everything from Julius Caesar's fire to Christian uprisings would be gone had the library contents been all destroyed.

In fact, the majority of the content that wasn't stolen by humans was moved to an alternate plane of existence and safeguarded. Berenice had been its guardian ever since.

Dr. Ma was able to move freely between varying planes of existence and enjoyed the ability to access the Library contents as needed for her job on Earth.

She and Allistair kept the location secure, allowing limited access to Otherworldly beings who could pass between the planes. So, practically nobody went there.

"Hello, Ma-sama," Berenice answered in her delicate voice. She sounded like chimes ringing each syllable of each word she spoke. Despite being ensconced in a stone figure, her Spirit was essentially a high level magical being.

Like Dr. Ma, she could transform from stone to a human guise rapidly and convincingly. Or, she could leave the stone that housed her and wander through other realms in an ethereal state.

Berenice was closer to human than Dr. Ma would ever be. But Ma was not magical. She, like David, was an Elemental. They were merely formed into this life by magic. Or science. Call it what you will.

Dr. Ma gently dipped the fingers of her left hand into the water of Bernice's fountain basin.

Immediately on contact, she was now standing in the great hall of the Library. The knowledge of the ages all around her was displayed in every form.

If you were human, and you could see into Dr. Ma's backyard, you would be convinced Dr. Ma had walked away from the fountain after gently dipping her hand in the water of the basin. You wouldn't exactly know where she went, but you would be sure she walked away.

If you were an Otherworldly being, you would have seen Dr. Ma dematerialize the instant her hand touched the water. You would not be able to see *where* she went. That would take great power and no other being on earth had that ability other than Allistair.

At this moment that is.

Berenice's fountain was also in the great hall of the Library. "Hello again, Berenice," Dr. Ma greeted her upon arrival.

"Hello, Ma-sama," Berenice said. Then the stone figure closed its lapis blue eyes and became still. And silent. She would wake at Dr. Ma's touch when she was ready to leave.

An excited squeak came from behind Dr. Ma and she turned, smiling at the Librarian who rushed up to greet her. "Ma-sama!" the elegant daimon greeted her.

"Maia my dear, you look well," Dr. Ma greeted the beautiful woman. Maia was a Greek nymph, the half breed child of the Greek deity Atlas and her nymph mother Pleione. She had taken the job as librarian long ago, to have something to occupy her mind. Immortality can be difficult at best.

"How is your son?" Dr. Ma continued. " I haven't seen him in ages. Hermes, Maia's son, was the messenger to the Gods in Greek and Roman times.

The Roman's called him Mercury. Since he was one of the only beings like Ma who could easily pass through planes of existence, Ma saw him as frequently as millennia of existence could accommodate.

Maia pouted, "Neither have I, he cannot pass here and he seems too busy to see his mother when I leave *briefly* to seek him out."

Maia looked at Dr. Ma sideways when she said the word, *briefly*. Ma knew she didn't want her to think she was slacking at her duties of librarian. "That's okay, Maia," Ma said soothingly. "You are welcome to some time off to see your son. If I needed you desperately I could easily find you."

Maia blushed slightly remembering the last time Dr. Ma had to 'find' her when she took some time off. The great dragon could zero in on you in no time. "Yes, well I prefer to be here," Maia said with an expansive sweep of her hand towards their surroundings.

"I wouldn't mind spending more time here myself," Ma said, staring hungrily at the books, scrolls, art and more modern items such as computer screens and tablets showing current events. There was even an entire case of People Magazines.

"You know you can subscribe to magazines online," Dr. Ma said to Maia, frowning slightly.

"Guilty pleasure," Maia replied, looking over towards her collection.

Dr. Ma rolled her eyes, mentally making note to discuss Maia's freedom in adding to the library, later. Not that there was limited space in the library. The place went on and on with no end.

The cool part of the design that she and Allistair had created was that you only needed to stand in one place and make your request. The I Library was as close to a living entity as it could be. Exactly how, was their secret.

After your request, the Library walls would shift, fold in on themselves and move every which way, before regurgitating the section or area you needed to look at. Right in front of you.

A reading chair, lamp, and table with a map light, would also appear with the section. That was Allistair's idea.

"Slight overkill," Ma thought. Often, she saw a glass of sherry and a decanter on a side table that appeared with Allistair's selections.

She sighed and turned to Maia. "I need," she had just begun when Maia interrupted her.

It's already coming," Maia said, proudly. "I have been paying attention to the activity in your area." Leaning in towards Dr. Ma conspiratorially, she said darkly, "I think it's who you believe it to be."

Dr. Ma was not surprised. If she was correct in what may have played a part in Joseph

McCarthy's sudden disappearance, Maia could have sensed its presence early on.

"Thank you, Maia," she replied as the section she needed settled into place in front of her. There was a tall stool, in front of what looked like a drafting table. On the table were a pair of white cotton gloves next to an ancient appearing tome.

The cover of the tome appeared to be some sort of skin. It also appeared to be moving slightly.

She knew the pages would be papyrus, dating from the early 700's BC. The skin was on many such works. Shed from Allistair himself in his transformed state, Maia had been crafting it into some type of magical protective layer for the most fragile works as long as Ma could remember.

"You know I don't need the gloves Maia," Ma said smiling. She was just going to slip gently into the document and look around. It was an odd transformation thing she could do.

The document existed in a sort of plane within a plane of existence. A sub world of information if you will. She didn't need to touch it to extract her information.

Maia sniffed and said, "It's a nice touch. We all know that using gloves is not done anymore, I just like the elegance of it."

"Just like Allistair's sherry," Ma thought. She knew that Maia was very modern for such an ancient deity. The romantic in her however, never changed through all her years of existence.

"Thanks, Maia," she replied. "I'll just be a minute."

Maia fixed her with a serious stare for a moment. "I will get the word out, if it is you know who again," she said. "You will get all the assistance you and David need."

"Thank you Maia," Dr. Ma acknowledged. "We won the last time but, always have all the odds on your side."

Maia nodded her agreement and glided away through the library wall.

"Walking around walls and through doors wouldn't hurt," Ma mumbled after her.

After all, the library was one big illusion. Why have it that way, if you were just going to glide through the wall and ruin the pretense?

Ma stood in front of the ancient text for a moment, pondering. This was an Akashic record. Different from the written or imagined pieces of literature in the Library, an Akashic record was a book about a being. Their life story, if you will.

The book had every moment of a being, human or Otherworldly's, existence, recorded chronologically. You just had to read the record for an up to date accounting of their actions. Thoughts were different. For that you had to get into their heads. The Akashic Record only kept track of actions they had taken, not why.

"First, Joseph McCarthy," Ma thought, reaching for a smaller, newer tome on the table. Holding it in her hand, Ma passed her spiritual being into the pages of his book. She focused on one week prior.

She would work her way to the current time and date slowly, looking for clues. This was slower than how she had obtained information in her last case. If the person was available and living, you could just siphon off their memories. She did this with one of her last case's killers.

Joseph McCarthy's past seven days came into focus. She saw the concern that he had after a phone call he received. She hoped she didn't have to go back further than a week.

He took actions to get his boat ready for a trip up the coast. His boat Captain arrived for instructions. Destination? Sag Harbor. The Captain left the McCarthy residence to begin preparations.

She watched the conversation between Joseph and his wife. So, Ann didn't know more than she was letting on. A sudden business trip, she had been told. It was Ann that packed for his trip herself, lovingly folding clothing and personal items into a small valise.

"Vuitton," Ma noted. Nice choice.

She watched McCarthy get driven to his boat in a dark colored Town Car and then she lost track of his movements. Entirely. Something completely obscured them. She hadn't even seen the Captain greet him. Or, oddly, any crew.

The record showed something else, but the missing time at the boat was of the most importance to her. Dr. Ma frowned and put down Joseph's record.

She looked at the ancient papyrus in front of her. "What have you been up to?" she thought. She hesitated before entering this record. That Otherworldly being was powerful. She would know that Ma was aware of all her actions when Ma entered her book.

Picking up another book instead, Ma opened it. This one was a log of sorts. She pulled out the coordinates Detective Brenner had given her. Fixing them in her mind, she entered the second book.

The log book was a record of the comings and goings of Otherworldly beings on the human plane of existence. On earth. If you didn't have exact coordinates, as well as the time and date correct, you would never find what you were looking for. It was a massive recording, and growing all the time.

She arrived at the time and place in seconds. What she saw confirmed her expectations. She remembered a strange Spirit Wind passing around her the day Joseph disappeared. It was faint. An Adept of some sort had just died. Suddenly. Not far away from where Ma had been.

Oddly, the Spirit was not seeking to enlighten her about its death. No 'message' was coming to her on the Wind.

She had the impression the Adept was assisting some entity to manifest on Earth, but that was all she had gotten. That, and the impression that the entity was a particular old foe or her's and David's. One she hoped not to deal with again anytime soon.

Dr. Ma and David had taken down this entity before. She thought they vanquished her hundreds of years ago. Dr. Ma put the log book down, next to Joseph's record.

She looked at the papyrus. "Your turn," she said grimly.

Chapter Four - Tam and Dr. Ma

Dr. Ma saw everything she needed for now in her trip to the Library. She didn't notice the entity's attention on her when she was inside her Akashic record.

Perhaps she could buy some time before Circe realized Ma knew she was involved. Circe would realize it eventually, but enough time may be given to investigate what the Sorceress had done.

She was back at Berenice's fountain in a few steps. Maia would give her grief the next time she visited for not saying goodbye, but time was pressing. Dipping her fingers into the lightly splashing water, she said, "I have to leave Berenice."

The little stone statue opened its eyes in surprise. Dr. Ma was not usually in a rush. "Yes, of course," Berenice replied. Ma found herself standing in the garden in moments. Hurrying back into the house she called for her djinn.

"David will be here tomorrow just before noon sometime. I will come home from the clinic for lunch. Please arrange to feed him before I get here," were her slightly terse instructions.

The djinn nodded and vanished before she could apologize for being curt.

She noticed the darkness that had crept up while she was in the Library. "It always took so much human time to be there," she thought. "That is why I seldom use the Library unless I really need it, or am not in a rush."

Walking into the kitchen, she found a light dinner waiting for her on the center island. The djinn had left it. "He is so efficient," she thought. She almost pitied David his antique djinn. "That is why the man eats at Renato's every day."

Finishing her meal more quickly than she would have preferred, she left the dishes and went to her dressing room to change into black training gear.

The fussy djinn would have a fit if she washed up. She had to insist on doing her own cleanup when she baked. That, or give him the day off. Not that he actually left the house, she just didn't call him. He often worked behind her back though.

Just as she finished changing she felt the security system alert her to an Otherworldly presence at the front door. It wasn't armed, just aware. A gentle knock on the door announced Tam's arrival. He was better at human rituals that she and David. She opened the door and let him in. The myriad of plants in Dr. Ma's house whispered softly to Tam as he walked into the center of the main room.

Smiling, Tam turned to her. "It's nice to be in a house like yours," he complimented Dr. Ma. "The plants in human houses are much less responsive."

Dr. Ma knew that was why Tam spent so much time riding off road on local mountain bike trails. The Otherworldly spirits in the parks and open areas were much more alive around him than around humans who couldn't see or communicate with them anyway.

"Are you ready to go?" Dr. Ma asked him.

"Yep," Tam answered. "What's the plan?"

"I will give you a lift if you don't mind," Ma said, "We are going to the last coordinates that our missing yacht was seen. The Jupiter Inlet area. When I set you down on the water there, will you just keep everything in balance and watch my back while I look around?"

"Sounds like fun," Tam replied, smiling. "I have always wanted to fly with you at least once."

Dr. Ma laughed. "Anytime Tam, let's do it again after this is over. I'm afraid I get a little hyper focused when I am working a case. It will be more fun for you when we are done investigating."

"Deal," Tam agreed. "Do you know what we are looking for?"

"Believe it or not, I think we are looking for traces that Circe may have been responsible for the disappearance," she said. Dr. Ma watched Tam's expression carefully for his reaction.

Tam's normal neutral expression shifted between anger and revulsion as Ma had expected. "*Her*? I really can't stand *her*," he said, almost spitting.

"No Wind or Air Spirit, nor Water ones, or even those that reside in animals, really liked Circe," Ma thought. "Hell, you could probably expand that dislike to a whole host of beings on any plane of existence she had visited."

Circe was the goddess of magic from ancient Greek mythology, in human history. Dr. Ma and Tam knew she was so much more now that she had a few millennia or more on her.

Age and experience developed skills better left to wither and die. Especially in her case. She never did anything good.

According to myth, she was created by Hecate, the goddess of magic and witchcraft, Circe became known in human literature sometime after 2000 BC. Ancient Greek Mythology wanders a bit.

Things got even worse when the Romans adapted and adopted the Greek gods.

Dr. Ma met Circe in battle centuries ago. Ma won. Circe was vanquished. Not gone mind you. Her magic had created a spiritual being that could not die. Otherwise how was she still hanging around?

It had not been pleasant, their encounter, and Dr. Ma had hoped, apparently futilely, that the minor goddess would stay vanquished for, if all went as planned, the length of human civilization.

Well, you could hope.

"Are you ready to go?" Dr. Ma asked Tam. They had walked out of Ma's back patio doors and made it halfway towards the wall of the Intracoastal Waterway. It was all her property down to the wall.

She grew a massive hedge of Florida Privet (Forestiera segregata) on both sides of her back yard. The dense shrubbery was almost eight feet high, running from the house to the concrete wall of the Intracoastal. As they walked, the hedges rustled, speaking to Tam and Dr. Ma.

"Yes, please," Dr. Ma affirmed, as the hedges seemed to darken and become even more impenetrable.

Tam grinned at her in the velvety darkness. South Florida had gorgeous evenings by the waterways. "I always forget how fluent you are in tree speak," he said.

A deep and slow voice came to them from the waterway north of where they stood. "She is quite fluent, young man," said Jamil. Ancient and powerful, Jamil was the guardian of a ley line running through Florida not far from where they stood.

"Jamil!" Tam called back joyfully in tree speak. "Long time, no see, Great One!"

"You could try riding by now and then," Jamil teased Tam. "My tree is out of the way for your speed demon riding group."

"He is right," Tam said to Dr. Ma. " I will go see him on my way home more often."

To Jamil, Tam said, "My apologies Great Guardian. I will visit you soon."

"Jamil is going to watch our passage tonight," Dr. Ma said to Tam. "He has been very awake lately, so, David and I involve him when we can."

"How interesting," Tam observed.

"Ready to fly?" Dr. Ma asked Tam. Tam nodded his assent and Ma grabbed him as she started running fast towards the Intracoastal Waterway. She was very powerful, even in human guise. Tam had forgotten just how powerful for a moment.

He was instantly reminded.

Taking a last stride, almost a leap up and over the short concrete barrier between her back yard and the waterway, Tam felt her transform. He heard the snap of the night air as her wings extended their full length. A strong downdraft first pulled at him then lifted him as she displaced the air around them with the beating of her massive wings.

He still felt her holding him gently to her chest, but she was no longer soft and human. Black, shiny skin, finely scaled, covered her. Her arms still resembled human arms, but her legs were those of her beast, large, and ending in razor sharp talons.

They climbed quickly into the night air. Tam could hear her in his mind now. "How are you doing?" she asked him. Her voice would be unintelligible to his mostly human ears if she tried to speak to him in her Elemental dragon form.

"Great!" Tam replied. He really was. Great that is. "This is awesome!" he thought. Ma headed north through the evening darkness after they were about three hundred feet up. As promised,

Tam called softly to the Wind Spirits around them to obscure their passage.

If you were human, you may see a quickly moving dark cloud pass overhead, but that would be all.

Arriving at the coordinates Detective Brenner has provided her with, Dr. Ma slowed to a stop in mid air. Powerful beats of her wings held them aloft as she looked down for the Wind Spirit that would support Tam while she searched the area.

"There," Tam pointed to what appeared to be a small wave crest in the middle of the Intracoastal Waterway. They were by the Jupiter Inlet. The water was calm. The soft glow of the Jupiter Lighthouse did not illuminate them where they were positioned.

Dr. Ma set Tam down carefully on the small wave crest. Tam stood there easily. It looked like he was surfing, but the little crest didn't move. In fact, the wave crest was just the breath of a Water Spirit, lifting the surface enough for Tam to balance above it.

"Neat trick," Ma sent mentally to Tam.

"I like it," Tam replied smiling. It wasn't hard to see Tam in the dark as Ma moved away from him to begin her search.

He had eyes like she and David did. Like all Otherworldly beings did. Lapis blue irises, but in the dark, a bright yellow ring for predators such as she was. As David was. Tam's eyes had a ring, but it was very faint. Wind Spirits were not predators.

Climbing up to 100 feet, Ma began her search. Elemental dragons had eyes like raptors. Dragons were part bird and part reptile. Unlike humans and other mammals, their eye is flatter with a circle of bony plates.

Four types of color receptors gave them the ability to see the color range humans could, but also ultraviolet light. Most could even see polarized light or magnetic fields.

When an entity like Circe passed in the earthly realm, they left trails of light particles. Depending on the strength of the creature, those telltale signs could be seen for years. Or centuries.

Dr. Ma wasn't taking any chances. She had felt the strange Spirit Wind that felt like Circe, a few days before Joseph McCarthy was reported missing. The signature was strong. That was what she was looking for now, evidence that Circe was behind this disappearance.

Tam kept his eyes on the dragon sweeping silently above him. Gently directing his Wind family to follow her path, he kept her obscured from human eyes while she worked.

"There," Dr. Ma said loud enough for him to hear. Startled, he almost slipped off the small wave crest. A mutter of protest came from the wind Spirit as it struggled to keep him aloft.

"Sorry," Tam said to the Wind Spirit.

Ma saw the telltale signature. Faint at first, it grew in strength the further out into the ocean it went. Then it just disappeared. Smack dab in the middle of the water. Gone.

Ma cursed softly under her breath and returned to Tam. She swept down to pick him up and they headed back towards her house.
Tam didn't ask if she was done, he knew she found what she needed. Thanking his Wind family for their help he gently waved his hands to dissipate the small wave crest.

A few minutes later, and Ma was dropping him gently onto her backyard lawn. She transformed fully as she landed herself. "Thank you Jamil," she called to the Guardian. There was no reply. Not one for small talk, he would have accepted her thanks and gone back to his endless pondering.

Tam and Dr. Ma walked slowly back to her open patio doors. "May I offer you a late night snack?" Dr. Ma asked Tam, waving her hand towards the kitchen as they entered. Tam could smell the aroma of a fresh pizza coming from that direction.

"I would say no," Tam smiled, "if you weren't such an incredible cook."

Ma laughed. "I'm afraid it is a lot healthier than what you eat every day at the shop. I put the oven timer on before we left and hoped that we would get back in the amount of time I expected to."

Ma quickly pulled the hot steaming pie from her custom wall oven and plated it. Pouring Tam a soda and her a glass of water, they both sat down in her ultra modern kitchen. The center island was the usual place for anyone to gather there and eat Ma's fabulous food.

Tam almost shoved a piece of the cheese and veggie laden pie into his mouth whole, he was so hungry. He suddenly realized he forgot to eat after the group bike ride earlier.

"Mmm delicious," he complimented her. "I know this isn't cheese and the crust is gluten free, but it's probably the best pizza I've had since the last time I was here."

"You know," Ma said around her own mouthful of pizza, "If you ate like this more often, your human body would thank you."

Tam laughed. "My wife doesn't cook and I don't have time to make this kind of food. When you start a chain, we will order from the shop." Ma laughed and then turned serious. She had finished her slice of pizza, and wasn't planning on a second, so she wouldn't compromise her digestion by talking about her findings.

"It was her," she said grimly. "Looks like she was guiding whomever or whatever was on the boat and then she, and whatever creature she brought with her, disappeared. I think I know where the boat is. She sent it way off course so it wouldn't be found too quickly."

"What is next," Tam asked. He was on his third slice of pizza. "Will you need me for anything else?"

"Not yet," Ma replied, frowning. "David should be home tomorrow and we will get with Detective Brenner to give him the whereabouts of Joseph's boat. There is nothing the human cops can do about finding him for now. David and I need to sit down and formulate a plan of attack."

"You know where to find me," Tam said, pushing back his chair and standing up.

"Would you like more to eat?" Ma asked.

"No thank you Ma-sama," Tam replied politely. "Three slices of pizza is more than enough, really. You must be thinking I am David. That boy can put away some food."

Ma laughed and accompanied him to her front door. "Yes, but I don't think the pizza would be of much interest to him unless he was starving."

"Tell him hello for me," Tam said as he left.

"Will do," Ma said softly to the empty night air. Tam was already gone. The faint light from his bicycle's taillight was rapidly disappearing north on Flagler Drive. Tam rode his bike everywhere. He only pulled out his shop van when he was transporting other bikes for customers or events.

Ma walked back through her quiet house. The plants were all whispering and chattering excitedly. "Yes, I know," Dr. Ma acknowledged them. "You love to see Tam." She smiled at them. The half human half Wind Spirit was a definite hit with her plant family at the house. She should invite him more often.

Walking back outside, she looked around her well laid out, slightly formal garden landscape. "I know you are here," Ma said softly. "I felt you when we got back."

Maia stepped out of the magnolia tree she was melding with to conceal herself. "I didn't want to startle the Wind Child," she said a bit guiltily.

Ma laughed. "He knew something was off, he looked right at you when we came back. Even I wasn't sure exactly where you were hiding."

"Is it her?" Maia stepped towards her, her face revealing her anxiety.

"Yes," Ma replied carefully. "Why are you so concerned about her being here? It is not as if you will have to deal with her. Right?"

"No, of course not," Maia said, turning away, twisting her hands together over and over. "I am just curious."

"Maia," Ma's tone of voice made the pacing entity jump and spin towards her.

"Don't shout!" Maia cried, placing her hands over her face. "I should have told you when I first knew something was going on."

"What are you trying to tell me," Ma continued darkly, not caring if she was increasing Maia's stress levels or not. Ma could be very intimidating when she focused on something. Or someone.

In answer, Maia held out an object to Dr. Ma. It appeared to be a small sphere, clear, with swirling shapes inside. The sphere was not however, an inanimate substance. It seemed to be a sheer layer of skin, or the outside layer of something living.

"How and why did you make this," Ma asked sharply. It was a Spirit Wind, trapped in an ectoplasmic expression, created by Maia. No small feat, it was trapping a psychic event in a piece of yourself, no matter how thin and transparent. It would remain fresh and intact in its living membrane.

'Reading' it later would release the information and set it free to deliver its message and move on.

"You were in the library and I stepped out for a moment, knowing everything would be safe with you there," she said, trying to get Ma's agreement with her reasoning.

"Go on," Ma said, her tone rather icy.

"Well, I think the Spirit Wind came looking for you," Maia raced on, trying to get the whole story out. "It was hovering by Berenice's fountain and I knew it couldn't get in to you in there so, I just wrapped it up for you."

Ma just stared. There was little to nothing that upset her after two thousand years here and an infinite time being Elemental before that to learn patience and calm.

Maia had probably saved a crucial piece of evidence for what Ma was sure would be another murder. Perhaps related to the recent disappearance she was investigating. She however, could not give Maia the idea the she approved of her methods.

"You could have come to get me," Ma offered, her expression stoney.

"Yes," Maia agreed, That would have been the better plan of course. Because shortly after I trapped it and put it in my pocket, I forgot all about it." Maia stopped talking and tried to offer her most ingenue type smile.

Ma frowned deeply. Before she could speak however, Maia thrust the small sphere into Ma's hand and simply disappeared. Ma looked down at in frustration.

She would have to wait until David got home. She didn't know the strength of the little sphere, and she didn't want to lose any important information.

She turned to call her house djinn, but he was already standing behind her bearing a silver tray like those once used to carry a presentation card from visitors to the master or mistress of the house they were visiting.

Ma sighed at his eccentricity and placed the sphere on the tray. At least it would be safe. He would be a perfect match for Maia with all his odd habits, if it was even possible. The djinn and the tray, promptly disappeared.

Chapter Five - Homecoming

The private jet landed at the General Aviation Center in Miami International Airport and disembarked its passengers.

Another dark SUV waited for them just off the tarmac. The Customs Agent met them at the plane. After a brief conversation with Allistair, the Agent stamped their passports and they were climbing into the waiting vehicle.

"No armed guards this time," Karen thought as she settled into the soft leather interior. David settled in beside her and Allistair took the seating across from them. The interior was outfitted more like a private limousine.

"Well kids," Allistair said jovially, "we will be home safe and sound in about an hour."

"How fast *is* your driver Allistair?" David said grinning.

"Fast enough," Allistair answered, sounding very happy.

David knew he was just happy that he had returned from South Africa with all of them intact. Dr. Ma would have no reason to be angry with the man. They all knew that she was easy to get along with, for the most part, but don't fail to do what she expected you to do. If you could avoid to that is.

"Drop me off please, at Dr. Ma's residence, and then take Karen home," David instructed Allistair.

"My thoughts exactly," Allistair agreed. "She will be waiting for you."

"My dear," Allistair addressed Karen, "will your mother be worried about you? I know Dr. Ma told her you were coming home today, earlier than expected."

Karen looked up suddenly. She seemed to have been deep in thought. "My mother?" Karen laughed lightly. "No, she won't be worried about me. My father worries, but he is out of town on a trip. I received an email from him before he left."

She frowned suddenly. "I don't have my phone, so I will have to ask Mother when he is due back. My phone was left at the campsite," she ended, trailing off.

David looked at Allistair. He noticed the man had not moved and was staring intently at Karen as she spoke. "I haven't been in touch with Dr. Ma either," he said carefully, watching for Allistair's reaction. Nothing. "I assume you have been keeping her updated on our trip and arrival?"

Allistair looked at him, pausing briefly before saying, "of course."

David stared at him intently. He was sure there was more to what Allistair was letting on. Looking over at Karen, he wondered if it was more for *her* sake. "What would involve Karen?" he wondered.

Karen was staring out of the window. She seemed to have lost her interest in flirting with him about halfway through their flight home.

"Figures," David thought. "Story of my life. Almost get the girl, scare the crap out of the girl, lose the girl, repeat."

When the SUV pulled up in front of Dr. Ma's residence, David jumped out quickly. Karen looked at him like she wanted to say something but, she stayed quiet.

"Call me if you need anything," David said to her and closed his door. He watched the SUV drive away. "That was some smooth talking," he thought. "No wonder you are alone."

David sighed and walked up to Dr. Ma's front door. He touched the rune on the side of her door briefly and it opened. He had no key to make it look normal to any human watchers. Shit happens.

The house felt strangely empty. Ma definitely wasn't on the premises. Mort, not his real djinn name, drifted up, smiling.

"Good day, Great Tiger," the djinn said cheerfully.

David couldn't help smiling. Mort was always so upbeat, it was hard not to. How the djinn came to name himself Mort and why he was always so damn cheerful David didn't really know. "Is Dr. Ma expected soon?" he asked the djinn.

"Oh, she is on the way Great One, she is coming from the clinic now," the djinn said. The floating figure bowed and started to drift away.

"Wait," David called after him The djinn stopped and looked at him inquisitively. "Has she left yet?" He was wondering if he should wait for her or go home. He was starting to get hungry. Home and a meal at Renato's sounded tempting.

"Yes, she has," Mort replied. " I was also instructed to have a repast available for your arrival Great Tiger. It is in the kitchen, waiting for you."

"Mort, please just call me David."

The djinn rolled his eyes. "Never," he stated dramatically. "Please help yourself," a slightly wispy looking hand swept towards the kitchen entrance. The djinn was trying to dematerialize. "I have some pressing matters to take care of, call if you need anything."

"Somehow," David thought, "I have heard that recently." His stomach growled and he headed for the kitchen to refuel.

He had not eaten nearly enough on the whole trip, especially after the massive amount of calories and energy expended on the whole debacle at the campsite.

A large bowl of steamed vegetables, fragrant with herbs waited next to a plate of fresh fruit and another plate of mixed raw seeds and nuts. Sighing with relief to be eating his preferred fare again, David sat at the center island of Dr. Ma's gleaming kitchen. Modern appliances, deep black granite and highly polished ebony wood created the well designed space.

He perched on one of her bar stools and began polishing off what had been left for him at an alarming rate. Never a worry about indigestion, he could consume just about anything that didn't eat him first.

In plant based foods that is. In a pinch he would substitute fish for a protein, but he hadn't eaten another animal's flesh or milk in as long as he could remember.

Well, there was that gardener, but it wasn't a planned meal after all.

The bar stool seat was made of one piece of carved, reclaimed wood from the same online store Dr. Ma bought her unusual agate, wood and stone plate wares. She preferred the 'energy' of natural products she had told him.

He couldn't agree more. He ate with his hands while in her kitchen or at home, deftly manipulating the food without need for utensils.

Metals bother him to eat with, but in public it was necessary.

David paused to see Berenice, the fountain spirit in Dr. Ma's backyard watching him as he ate. A slight flush crossed his cheeks as he remembered her telling him once, that it was very sensual watching him eat with his hands.

"Honestly, she was an ancient in Spirit form occupying a stone statue. Where did she expect to go with such a comment?" he thought.

Finishing his meal, he stood to put the dishes in Ma's oversized double bowled modern sink. Instead of steel, it was made of some dense, veined granite. Highly polished it always appeared like it had never been used.

Mort appeared at his shoulder in a moment. "She is here," Mort announced in his dramatic tone. "Shoo," he said, flicking his hands at David to go away.

"You should know better that to think Mort would let you do dishes in my home," Ma's voice came from the archway joining the kitchen and the great room in the center of the house.

"Of course NOT," Mort affirmed, turning his back on David and starting to run steaming water into the deep granite sink.

David turned to see Dr. Ma standing there, staring at him. Her arms raised up to invite him, and he was across the room hugging her in a split second. He experienced his usual rush of intense feeling when they touched. If Ma felt the same, she never let on.

"Hello child," she said softly in his ear. "Welcome home."

He held her a moment longer, letting the grief and anxiety of the last several days flow away as her calming energy washed over and through him. He knew she was healing his pain with her powerful Qi expression.

When his relief began to feel more like arousal, he let her go and stepped back.

She smiled her all knowing smile at him and said, "Lets sit outside, it's a beautiful day."

David agreed, following her lead as she headed out the back patio doors. Dr. Ma's home was made up of glass panels on the entire east side facing the Intracoastal Waterway. The doors were also glass, framed and hinged, then reinforced to hurricane and storm standards.

Not that they needed to be. The dragon was like the rhinoceros years ago in the Miami Metro Zoo. The animal had just stood there during a major hurricane that leveled everything around for miles. In her case, her energy would protect her entire home and garden.

The view was breathtaking into her extensive and over planted garden. Tall privet hedges along the north and south sides maintained privacy as well as a perfect growing environment for her plants and trees.

Passing Berenice's statue in the merrily splashing fountain waters, David looked back to find her slanted blue eyes checking him over with a slightly lascivious smile on her stone features.

"Really Berenice," Ma commented without ever looking up from where she was going. "Where do you think that will get you with the tiger?"

"What I said," David muttered, following Ma to the large swinging bench that faced the waterway. Deeply shaded by several varieties of sweet smelling vines laden with colorful flowers, the bench almost had an air of silence around it when you sat there.

"Yes," Ma answered his unspoken question. "I finally warded it for privacy. Keep that in mind if you visit when I am not here."

She spoke a word softly before they sat down. He couldn't quite make out what she said. "You may get a nasty shock if you don't release the ward first."

"I assume you won't be telling me what you said?" David asked, sure she would absolutely not be telling him.

"Consider it a challenge to learn a new skill," Ma answered, laughing. She sat gracefully on the bench that appeared to David to be made of thick woven vines. "By the way, I had Winnie clear the patient schedule for the rest of the day."

David sat beside her. "Thank you," he said wearily. The bench was always comfortable, the woven branches gave slightly with your weight, eliminating the need for cushions.

"Detective Brenner will be joining us shortly. We have a body to recover, left by an old foe," she said looking out at the waterway. "Joseph McCarthy has been missing for a few days," she added.

David sat up straight, his fatigue forgotten. "What?" he asked, and then quickly added, "Is Allistair going to stay with Karen?" He knew that Karen would be given the news when she arrived home.

"Yes, of course he is," Ma answered him. "Jeremy is also there. I told him she would be arriving shortly and he went there first to help her mother deliver the news. I met Ann," Ma continued. "I see that she and Karen are not close?"

"No," David answered. "Karen is adopted. Ann wasn't able to have children naturally."

"Ann is too thin to have conceived," Dr. Ma said with a light frown. "You have seen this before in patients."

David nodded his agreement. A woman being very thin did not make her infertile per se. In Traditional Chinese Medicine, the theory was, the mother had to have an acceptable vessel for the child to seat itself in the womb.

Undernourishment can lead to problems carrying the child to term, not in conceiving.

"Tam and I went to the last coordinates that Joseph's boat was seen yesterday. He disappeared right after leaving the Jupiter Inlet. I found his missing boat, hung up in that little island grouping we have seen before. The one about halfway between the Florida coastline and the Bahamas."

David sat up even straighter. "What?" The island grouping was definitely Otherworldly. Mariners and planes would pass it without noticing the small grouping was there. It could even 'shift' its position if a vessel was heading straight towards it.

They both believed they knew the creator of the island grouping. But, they hadn't heard from him in centuries.

"No way," David said. "Wait, what do you mean, hung up?"

"It was as if the islands were grouped around it, holding it there," Ma said thoughtfully. "At least that is the impression I got."

"So you're going to send Brenner there to retrieve it?" David said.

"Not exactly," Ma answered him. "When I landed on board to see what was up, the little islands shifted and let the boat loose. I must have broken the spell holding it there. It's drifting."

"Joseph?" David asked hesitantly.

"No sign of him," Ma said, shaking her head in the negative. "One body, the Captain by the looks of the clothing, and one blood stain that may have been a crew member. It didn't smell like Joseph."

"So," David said, "One dead, a probable conspirator with her and one bloodstain is all that's left of a snack? For whom or what?"

"That is how I see it too," Ma said. "I don't know what she had with her that needed the snack. The body looked older than the time Joseph has been missing so, conspirator yes and most likely one of her soulless waking dead. I really hate that little trick of hers."

"This should be an interesting one for Brenner," David said as he watched the usual Intracoastal

Waterway traffic go by. Boats of all shapes and sizes passed along the stretch they were facing. "Do you think Circe had Joseph in her sights or is this random?"

"Argh!" Mort said from next to him suddenly. "Don't say that witch's name out loud, even in Ma's little garden cone of silence! Are you crazy? She can hear you in the next plane of existence."

"Hey!" David said, recovering himself from the surprise of Mort's sudden appearance. "Can't you just walk up like a normal butler, or whatever you are supposed to be, instead of just materializing out of thin air?"

"I am a djinn," Mort said with exaggerated dignity. "We don't just *walk up.*"

"Make some noise then," David said.

"Like you make noise when you walk up," Ma laughed.

"Yes, okay, point taken," David said smiling.

Mort cleared his throat to get their attention, "Detective Brenner is here to see you. He is in the kitchen helping himself to whatever food we may have left." He looked pointedly at David and disappeared. A disembodied voice came from where he was last seen. "Oh, and Allistair arrived and went right to the library."

"Thank you, Mort," Dr. Ma said. She rose from the garden bench and looked at David seriously. "She really does have incredible hearing, let's avoid saying her name unless it's necessary."

David nodded his agreement and followed her into the house, where Jeremy Brenner was halfway through one of Dr. Ma's muffins. He had taken two on a paper towel from the clear glass storage plate and was sitting at the center island. Crumbs were escaping everywhere. David grinned at the site. "Mort should be having a silent hissy fit right now watching this," he thought."

He knew Mort watched everything that went on in that house and making a mess all over his spotless kitchen would be just killing him. Especially since he couldn't simply materialize and clean up. Not with Detective Brenner in the residence. Djinn could be seen by humans when they are solid enough to clean up a kitchen mess.

Brenner lifted a muffin towards Dr. Ma and mumbled through the mouthful, "You don't mind?" or something like that.

Dr. Ma laughed. "Jeremy, please eat whatever you want. I interrupted your lunch break to come here, so, tell me what else I can get for you."

Jeremy Brenner shook his head in the negative. "No thank you," he said more clearly after swallowing his bite of muffin. "I didn't have time for lunch today anyway. I just left the McCarthy residence."

"How are they doing?" David asked.

"Not a happy household," Brenner replied grimly.

"I found Joseph's boat," Dr. Ma told him. She held up her hand as he started to talk around another bite of muffin. "Joseph is not on board but I think his Captain's body is there. If there was a crew member, all that is left of him seems to be a large amount of blood."

Brenner took all this in, chewing thoughtfully. "Where is the boat now?"

"Adrift," Ma answered, handing him a piece of paper. "These are the last coordinates.

Brenner took the information and pulled out his phone to make a call. A few minutes later, he hung up. "They will find it pretty quickly," he said. "Condition of the body?"

"Deteriorated," Ma answered.
Brenner nodded and pushed back from his now crumb strewn place at the center island. "I will let you know what we get when we have the boat gone over."

Neither Dr. Ma nor David were surprised that he no longer seemed interested in how they obtained information on cases. "Any ideas on Joseph's whereabouts?"

"Not yet, Jeremy," Dr. Ma said, "but I am working on it."

"Thank you for the muffins," Brenner said as he let himself out the front door. "Delicious, as always, Dr. Ma."

When the door closed, a distinct sound of cursing and grumbling could be heard from the kitchen. Mort was cleaning up Jeremy's muffin mess.

"I'm going to join Allistair in the library," Dr. Ma said to David. "Why don't you go lie down in my spare room and get some rest?" I don't want you out of my sight yet. Not while you are tired and she is on the loose."

David was going to object, but the tenderness in her voice stopped him. He nodded and smiled at her before walking down the hallway to the guest room she always had ready for him. Rest sounded beyond good.

Hurrying outside to Berenice's fountain she dipped her hand in the water and was suddenly standing in the library. "What?" Berenice said to her, "No tiger?"

"I am afraid he needs to rest dear," Ma said, smiling at the statute. Bringing David into the library was possible for Ma, but it caused him a lot of energy expenditure to maintain his Elemental essence in the alternate plane of existence she and Allistair had created there.

She wouldn't bring him if he was tired unless it was necessary.

Berenice pouted slightly. "Oh, of course," she said. "Another time then."

Dr. Ma started to move away to find Allistair and then turned back. "And no leaving the statute to go find him," she warned. We are down here and he needs sleep. You keep watch."

She and Allistair could come and go without her help, but she guarded the entrance against any intruders strong enough to get in as well as making their comings and goings much simpler.

"I wouldn't leave you here unprotected!" Berenice said indignantly.

"Good," Dr. Ma said and walked away.

A little squeak of excitement preceded Maia's rushed arrival. "Ma-sama!" she said, looking expectantly over Ma's shoulder. "Is David with you? I thought I heard him, or um, heard he may come down," she said, fumbling her words.

"You have got to be kidding me," Ma thought as she stepped around her. "This is out of control."

Aloud, she said, "No Maia, David is upstairs resting and you," Ma said pointedly, "are needed here in the library."

Maia looked startled as Dr. Ma all but read her thoughts on the subject. "Yes, of course," she

120

said, trying to give the impression she was not just looking forward to David visiting the library like a giddy school girl. "I was just coming to take you to Allistair."

Dr. Ma rolled her eyes behind the beautiful entity's back at Maia saying she needed to guide Ma through a Library that responded to your every need.

Maia led the way for the moment that the library took to rearrange itself around them. Allistair was sitting in a gilt armed, velvet flocked chair with a sherry in one hand and an open book dating from several centuries ago in his lap. He looked up as she entered.

"Ma-sama," he greeted her jovially. "I think I found something," Another chair, a match to his own, glided into place at his side. She said down to look at the book he was holding.

"*Appearances of the Sorceress*," she read the title and looked down at the page his finger was pointing to. "Last seen in France, 14th century, Duchy of Aquitaine, Bordeaux. Where did you get this?" Ma asked, picking up the slender tome to see the author. "Ah, the astrologer, Monsieur Lake."

"I had him track her after you and David dispatched her so efficiently the last time," Allistair said. "This was just before you two took her out. She hasn't been seen since, and Lake misses nothing that manifests here on earth."

Yes," Ma agreed, "he is good. Have you been in contact with him lately?"

"I missed his last quarterly email of World astrological predictions, going after your wayward tiger," Allistair began. Ma gave him a dark look. "Okay, okay," he said. "But he did notify me of her reappearance, roughly coinciding with the South Africa trip and Joseph's disappearance. Lake pinpoints her return occurring in Palm Beach itself. On the island."

"Yes," Ma agreed. "That fits, but I don't know much more right now. I brought you something that may answer some questions."

She held out, what appeared to be a piece of decomposing flesh. The skin was barely attached to it. The smell was atrocious as she held it out, unwrapped from the plastic that had been hiding its presence up until now.

"Lovely," Allistair intoned. He carefully took the offering from her. Making a face that clearly said he was disgusted, he quickly swallowed the piece of rotting flesh and followed it with a large sip of sherry.

Elementals can identify energy patterns by mingling their essence with organic items. Allistair and David could both consume a bit of organic matter and identify almost everything about it as it merged with their own molecules.

Ma would have to have immerse her spiritual energy in the putrid bit of the Captain's flesh. Based on how it smelled, Allistair's method was the better choice.

After a minute, and several more sips of sherry from his refilled glass, Allistair was ready to divulge what he had found out. "Ok," he said. "First of all, it was the Captain. He called the sorceress to, of course, gain power and wealth in his human life. In exchange was the usual gift to her of his soul and life force."

"Why does anyone believe that will actually happen?" Ma interrupted him. She was making more of a statement than asking a question, but Allistair answered her anyway.

"Nobody is ever left to tell the truth to the next idiot and, one or two actually get the deal and write about it in their little black magic grimoires," he opined. "Well, until she killed them right after they wrote it."

"Exactly," Ma said.

"Then she re-animated him. I really hate that trick of hers. She was supposed to have him take Joseph onboard and deliver him to her, if I read the prediction correctly," he concluded.

"Crew was a snack?" Ma pressed for more information.

"A Cetus ate someone," Allistair answered. "Must have been her transportation to the boat. You know she is weaker over water. But no, it looks like Joseph added two to the party. One was probably the snack, one looks like it may still be around. One crew member was planned but became dead prematurely. No Wind?"

Ma suddenly thought about the trapped Spirit Wind that Maia had given her. "Possibly, I will have to check."

"There was a second crew member but I think he bailed early on from the trip. He should be alive and able to give some background on the whole mess. If you can find him." Allistair finished with a sigh. He took a big swallow of sherry. "No more rotting flesh snacks for awhile, okay?"

"Yes," Ma agreed. "Well, thank you Allistair, now all we have to do is find her, find Joseph, and hopefully take her out for another few centuries."

Chapter Six - All In A Day's Work

They followed Ma's morning run route, discussing what she and Allistair had come up with in the Library. Ma also went over all the information she had obtained in his absence.

David had stayed in a deeply meditative state until the next morning. Knowing he needed the rest, and having a dangerous ancient sorceress in the area, Ma had not disturbed him.

Circe was well documented in Greek mythology as a sorceress, but, was far older. An ancient entity had formed her, no doubt for a less than honorable purpose, and she had existed ever since. She liked all the attention she received from the Greeks and so kept the name Circe. She also kept Circe's reputation for evil doing.

Dr. Ma and David had faced her more than once, but most memorably in 14th century France, where they had vanquished her. At least for awhile.

You cannot destroy matter, only change it. Basic physics principle, folks. Now she was back again. "But, why target Joseph?" they both asked simultaneously as they continued north along County Road past Trump's place on their left.

Dr. Ma ran easily next to David, his pace slightly slower than his normal blistering speed, her route longer today as she headed towards his apartment in downtown Palm Beach.

Not that it mattered much to their human bodies. Elementals pass on much to their human selves. Either could run just as fast or just as long if they wished to.

Before they left on the run, Ma had siphoned off a bit of Maia's trapped Spirit Wind. The whole vision would have to wait until later. She now knew the location of the first missing crew member.

He wouldn't be giving Detective Brenner any information.

She would call the detective later today and tell him where to recover the body. The blood smear was also identified for her. At least one Miami criminal was never going to be located.

You disappear forever when eaten by mythical sea creatures.

"Let's visit your place and then go back to mine to change for work," Dr. Ma said. "You can see everything is fine and say hello to your charges." She meant his ancient djinn housekeeper and his beautiful orchids.

David knew Ma was right about him staying with her until they took care of Circe. She was dangerous. "Okay, no problem, can we run by Karen's just to see if everything looks," he hesitated, searching for the right word. "Undisturbed?"

"Sure," Dr. Ma said. It was early but he was indicating a check of non human presence in the area. She was proud of him for his cautious approach. The tiger was a bit of a headlong rush into battle guy.

They reached the front of the McCarthy residence just as light was breaking over the island. The front door opened and Karen stood there with Detective Brenner.

Both Elementals stopped still suddenly. There was something intimate about the closeness of the two humans standing in the doorway.

"Thank you Jeremy," Karen was saying. Her voice was clear to their sharp Otherworldly ears. She handed him a mug of what smelled like coffee to Dr. Ma and David's extra sensitive noses.

Bending towards him, she kissed him gently on the lips. Brenner looked startled for a moment and then quickly kissed her back. Moments later he was getting into his unmarked police car in her front drive and leaving.

Karen stared after him, pausing, and then closed the door.

David hadn't moved a muscle since they suddenly stopped running when the front door opened. If Ma was hearing correctly, she wasn't sure he had even taken a breath.

Now, he turned away from the McCarthy home and resumed their run in the direction of his own small apartment off Worth Avenue.

Ma followed him quietly. She said nothing as he chose the back way, from Peruvian, up his flight of stone stairs and into the cool, calming front room.

David checked around quickly and misted the orchids who were chattering in their excitement to see him. He shushed them, seeing his ancient djinn was still sleeping. Exiting with Dr. Ma behind him, he locked the front door and touched the security ward next to the door jamb.

They ran back along Flagler Drive this time. First they went north briefly and up and over the Okeechobee bridge.

David seemed to pick up speed as he went. She touched his arm to remind him to slow down. One, two, three, four, five strides to one breath. Ma figured they were clocking about a 5 minute mile. No real stress for the Elementals, but you had to be careful about startling the humans out at this hour.

Anything faster would have caught too much attention.

South on Flagler past all the exercisers and their pets they raced. Jamil was a blur. The guardian may not have even noticed their passing, his reactions were so slow. When they finally reached her house, she grabbed his arm. "David," she said softly.

He looked at her, his sadness almost palpable. He opened his mouth to speak but closed it without uttering a sound.

"She is safe, the house was clear, and I am sure Detective Brenner was seeing to their safety personally," Ma said. She realized too late that what she said sounded insensitive.

"I'm sorry, I didn't mean that exactly as it came out," she tried to correct herself.

"It's fine," David said in a strained voice. "We didn't have anything going really." He spoke less than truthfully. It didn't matter, Ma knew his thoughts completely.

"She looked happy, and she is human of course," he continued. "Nothing with me would ever work out well for her."

David turned away and opened Ma's door with just the touch of the security ward. Dr. Ma looked over her shoulder to make sure no human neighbors were watching. The coast looked clear.

She followed him in and let the subject go. Nothing good could come of the direction this conversation was taking.

They had a quick breakfast after they had showered and changed. Driving to work in silence they were both deep in thought. Winnie was waiting for them when they came in the back door.

"Welcome back!" Winnie greeted David.

He stopped, waiting for the sarcasm, her usual method of communicating with him. Nothing. She just stood there waiting for his reply. "Okay, what is wrong with Winnie?" he said, turning to Dr. Ma. "Did you change her herbal formulas while I was gone?"

Winnie tapped her foot and pointed at him, "I missed you," she said, "Go ahead and be a smart ass and I will make sure it doesn't happen again."

"Now, there's my girl," David said in mock relief, bending to place a quick kiss on her cheek as he passed. She quickly swatted him as he went by. Dr. Ma, ahead of David looked back as Winnie made contact with David's right side.

She noticed he made a slight wince in pain.

Ma grabbed his arm and pulled him into her office, closing the door. "What hurts? Why do you look like you are in pain?" she asked.

David looked at her sideways and pulled out his tucked in Brooks Brother's fitted no iron shirt. He unbuttoned the front and pulled back the right side.

Dr. Ma saw a bruise blossoming over his ribcage. "Where did you get that?" she asked incredulously. She and David could be injured, but they healed quickly.

She had been with David pretty much straight through since he retuned from South Africa. Long enough for him to have healed from anything prior to that. Like at the campsite debacle.

"I don't know," David answered her. "I felt something hit me during the attack in South Africa," he said. "It left a mark that just never really went away, and now the bruise is getting bigger. Allistair noticed it on the plane and told me to show you."

Ma grimaced but said nothing. She gently touched the surface of the bruise and David's body jerked in pain. He didn't move away from her, despite his discomfort, as she continued her inspection.

Ma was using her Qi to explore the injury and it's origin. She pulled her fingers away and cursed under her breath.

"What?" David said somewhat apprehensively. Ma didn't curse over nothing.

"Just something Allistair found in the library," she answered, evasively.

"Come on," David said frowning, "just tell me."

"I will tell you more when I am sure," Ma said firmly. "For now, I am going to have to treat that before it gets worse. I wish you had said something sooner."

"I'm sorry," David replied, "I didn't want to worry you any further."

Ma made an exasperated sound. "Can you work with it today?" she asked.
"We will have to be alone for me to treat it."

A slight shadow passed across David's features as she said this. "So, it's an Otherworldly injury?" he asked. "You and Allistair think there was something non human in the group that attacked us in South Africa?"

"Yes," Ma replied. "I think you didn't notice in all the, ah, activity."

David nodded his head. "I wouldn't have. Did I kill it?" he asked.

"Allistair's people found only humans in the body count. It could have been a human controlled by an Otherworldly or just wielding a special weapon," Ma answered.

David suddenly looked up, it was dawning on him who his two friends may be considering as responsible for the attack at the tiger reserve. "*Her*?" he said in a strained voice, almost a low growl.

"Now that I see your injury," Ma said, reaching for her cell phone, "I will have to speak to Allistair. He was thinking that way."

David nodded and fixed his clothing so he could start seeing patients. "I will get started on the day," he said. "There isn't a class tonight, so after Winnie leaves, we should be undisturbed."

"I will have Allistair join us if he can," Ma replied.

Winnie was waiting in the hallway when David emerged. She knew that when Dr. Ma closed her door fully it was as good as a 'Do Not Disturb' sign, no matter how many patients were on the books.

She pointed at Room One in her quiet way of indicating the first patient to be seen. Winnie hated keeping anyone waiting. It was a pet peeve.

David walked into Room One to begin the day.

Hours later, and a hurried lunch of David's snacks to keep them going, they had finally caught up on the backlog.

Dr. Ma was manipulating the partial subluxation of a proximal tibiofibular joint for a Polo player. The rider had been crashed into by another horse and rider with sufficient force to injure the joint but not enough to require surgery.

David came in to the treatment room to help her hold the repaired joint in traction while she injected and wrapped it. The player was due to compete in a national tournament in 3 days. His team was expected to win.

"Dr. Ma, will I be able to play?" he asked.

"Of course," Ma answered. He had only winced slightly as she manipulated and stabilized his left knee.

She knew that after spending most of his adult life at the top of his field, little would keep him from playing well in the competition if he was able to get on his horse.

"Absolutely *do not* unwrap my tape job," Ma said firmly. "Leave your high boots on at all times, live in them really."

The player smiled, straight white teeth in a handsome dark skinned face with a shock of black hair, the usual slender, but heavily muscled body, reminded Dr. Ma why this sport was so popular in the media.

Handsome players and stunning horses, both with rippling muscles, made for good press.

"Whatever you say, I haven't been able to walk properly for three days since it happened," he said.

"It will take a couple months to fully heal," Ma warned. "Wrap it every day the way I showed you and if you have any further problems, we will re-evaluate."

Ma left the room to get his herbal prescription for pain and inflammation from the pharmacy. The handsome young man looked at David, smiling, and said, "She is something else, right?"

"You have no idea," David said, needling a few points to enhance the healing effect of the treatment. "You will have to come by for a followup injection if you are still in pain the morning of the competition."

The player seemed not to hear him as he looked towards the door. "Is she single?" he asked.

David laughed. This was a new one. Usually Ma intimidated more that interested. He was at least half her human age! "Yes," David answered. "But, she doesn't date patients."

The player laughed. "Not for me, my finance wouldn't go for it. I was asking for my brother. He is in town from Chile for the tournament."

"You can ask her," was all David replied, smiling to himself. "Okay, you are all set. Use the crutch she gave you to keep weight off the leg and have someone help you into and out of the saddle when you ride."

David knew that the majority of their advice to the player would not be followed. "Good luck on the National Championship," he said.

"Thank you," the player answered as he hurriedly hopped out front on his crutch to speak with Dr. Ma.

The door chimed shortly after the player left, disappointed that Dr. Ma was not available to meet his brother before he left. She did tell him to have his brother call her if and when he returned to the States this year.

The front door chime rang as Allistair walked in. Meticulous three piece suit and tie notwithstanding, the man was always a picture of perfection.

Winnie greeted him and locked up behind him. She always thought that if her dear Bud ever pre-deceased her, and if she was still in fighting shape, she would make a play for that man.

"Winnie, my dear," Allistair greeted her, placing a box of her favorite Godiva truffles on the front desk. "I hardly get to see you anymore as hard as Dr. Ma works you!"

Winnie smiled and took her present. She used to go to Allistairs office with paperwork from the clinic. He always took her to lunch on those days. Now, with ever increasing technology and their new computer guy, she rarely had to interact with Allistair.

"Thank you for the chocolate, Allistair," Winnie said smiling. "Maybe I will come work for you instead."

"Don't even joke," Allistair said dramatically raising one eyebrow. "Dr. Ma would have my skin if I stole you." Still attached to my body he thought after he said it.

Winnie patted him on the arm and said, "They are in the dojo, waiting for you." She thought the location of their meeting was a bit odd, but she said nothing.

Allistair walked out the back door and through the attached Zen garden into the dojo. He smiled at the figure of Hotei as he passed the small stone Buddha.

Dr. Ma had a mat of some type of grass in the center of the dojo floor. Incense swirled through the air and a few large candles stood in tall holders in the corners of the room. It took the

Elemental snake only seconds to note the location of the only inhabitants of the room. He didn't have to see them to know everything about them. His tongue touched his human lips briefly, gathering information from the air.

"Come in Allistair," Dr. Ma said walking towards the mat she had prepared. "David?" she asked over her shoulder. "Ready?"

David came forward and lay down on the grass mat. He wore nothing but a small, snug pair of black workout shorts. Allistair's human heart gave a quick skipped beat response to the site of David's beautiful human form.

Elegant and unusual tattoos wrapped his waist and dove down his hips into the snug black shorts. His powerful musculature was rippling in the candlelight under tight skin and almost no body fat.

"You are so much better looking in skin instead of fur," Allistair remarked. The attorney was definitely bi-sexual. He had found the tiger a distraction for the thousand years he had known him.

David smiled at him in the dim light, white teeth flashing, yellow rimmed blue eyes just barely showing. It wasn't fully dark in there, so he didn't need the brighter glowing yellow iris ring yet to see.

"Really?" David teased. "Sure, hit on me when Ma is going to incapacitate me, instead of when I can do something about it."

Both were trying to break the tension. They had a good idea of what was coming. If David had been wounded internally by an Otherworldly, it was not going to be pleasant for Dr. Ma to heal it. It was going to get ugly.

"Lie down and let's get going on this," Ma said interrupting their banter. She was a bit anxious to see what had happened to David. She was even more stressed about the pain she was about to cause him.

David lay down in the center of the grass mat, head pointing north, feet south and arms by his sides. He had broken out in a light sweat, anticipating what was to come.

Dr. Ma and Allistair knelt on either side of him, her representing the East and he the West.

The backdoor opened and Tam walked in, shedding his bike gear as he went. "Sorry I'm late," he apologized.

Dr. Ma gave him a look. "South, please," is all she said. Tam knelt down by David's feet. They were only missing a North position by his head, but that couldn't be helped.

"I didn't know Tam was coming," David said, anxiety increasing with the addition of another Otherworldly to help. "Hey Wind man," he said.

"Hey big guy," Tam answered.
"Allistair and I are being cautious," Ma said in explanation. "We don't know all the Sorceresses new tricks. "Ready to begin?"

David nodded wordlessly and closed his eyes. All three looked down at the dark bruise, now spreading over most of his side and creeping into his lower abdomen.

Dr. Ma placed her hand gently, palm down on the center of David's bruise and said what sounded like "Eh, no may." There were no words in any language to correlate with the sounds she made.

The sounds she produced had existed long before human language.

David's body stiffened. He gave a grunt of pain. His body broke out in a heavier sweat and he bit his lip to stifle further complaints. Ma worked her hand slowly over the bruised area.

A soft luminous glow lifted from David's bruised tissue, surrounding her hand. He twisted in pain despite his best efforts not to move for her. A strangled cry escaped his mouth. Ma knew the pain was increasing.

"Allstair, Tam," Ma directed, "Hold him please."

The stocky man in the meticulous suit lifted Davids' upper body and wrapped his thick, muscular arms around the tiger's upper torso, pinning David's arms back away from where Dr. Ma was working. His powerful legs wrapped around Davids waist, locking them together.

Tam, slighter in build but very strong, locked his legs around David's and sat on them.

The two would still be no match for the tiger if he transitioned. Allistair's snake would be hard pressed without a head start. But David wasn't going to transition. The injury was obtained in the human realm, he would just have to suffer here.

Ma pressed on. Muttering under her breath, she pulled at the energetic signature buried in David's chest just under the ribcage. From the smell, she knew it was meant to be a slow acting poison.

Something or someone had tried to kill the tiger in South Africa. Something other than the men with guns.

David screamed suddenly as she pulled hard, and Allistair slapped a meaty hand over his mouth to muffle the sound. David's body now struggled in pain, soaked with sweat.

His scream was muffled but audible in the attached clinic. Winnie was talking to Detective Brenner, who had come by to give Dr. Ma and David an update on the case. Brenner frowned and tried to walk out the back door to enter the dojo through the Zen garden.

Winnie stopped him. "No interfering Detective," Winnie said. "I must insist, some crazy martial arts thing that the big wigs are doing," she said in explanation.

It was a lie of course. She had no idea what they were doing.

Brenner knew a scream of pain when he heard one. Winnie wasn't fooling him, but the woman stood hands on hips, between him and the back door of the dojo. She pointed at the clinic back door and said, "Back you go, sit in the waiting room like a good boy."

Jeremy Brenner would have been insulted at being spoken to like that by anyone else *but* Winnie.

Another scream came, less muffled this time. Winnie all but shoved him though the clinic backdoor.

"Sh-t, she is strong!" he thought. He didn't argue with her, but he did give one last suspicious glance at the dojo back door.

If Dr. Ma or David were in trouble she wouldn't be trying to stop him from helping them.

Ma sensed the two of them there but couldn't do anything about it right then. "Did you lock the back door then you came in, Allistair?" she asked.

"No," the man struggling to restrain David's twisting torso said through grunts of effort. "I'm sorry."

"Nothing to do about it now," Ma replied, eyeing the door. "I think the resident pit bull, Winnie, took care of it."

She gave a final yank and quickly dropped the soft bit of tissue she had ripped out of David's chest on the grass mat. It glowed softly on its own.

"Bloodroot! Really?" Ma said scornfully. Sanguinaria canadensis poisoning was a painful way to die for an Elemental. Especially when it was placed internally and spelled to release its effect slowly.

She got up angrily, grabbed the glowing orb and froze it instantly with a puff of her breath.

"I didn't know you could do that without transforming," Tam said, slightly awed.

He and Allistair were gently untangling from David and placing him back down on the grass mat in a supine position. His breathing was still labored with soft grunts of pain and he hadn't spoken to them yet. Blood dripped from his lower lip. He had bitten through it in his pain.

"Well," Dr. Ma said, "There isn't much call for it when I am not transformed, really." She placed the frozen orb in her lab coat pocket and looked at them. "Stop gawking, apparently Detective Brenner is here to see me. I will see you two later. Thanks for your help."

"What about David?" Tam said, indicating David, still on the floor.

"Oh, he'll be up soon," Allistair said, answering for Dr. Ma. "Leave him be."

Dr. Ma nodded her agreement. "He is safe here. He will heal quickly now."

The three left out the back door. Tam took off on his bike and Allistair got into the back of his black Cadillac Escalade. His driver had been waiting for him while he was in the dojo.

Ma stood for a moment before entering her clinic back door. She loved the well appointed garden that framed the rear entrances, separating it from the parking area.

Orchids and other flowering vines draped the wood lattice work that Terry, one of her Ironman athlete patients had painstakingly built.

The small statue of Hotei that Allistair had greeted watched silently over the area.

In Buddhism, he was known as the happy Buddha. His visage was based on the stories of an eccentric Zen monk who lived over 1,000 years ago.

The little burlap sack , open at his feet, was given a fresh offering of fruit daily. The birds and lizards who could enter the tiny slats of the garden enclosure ate them. They were gone every morning.

Hotei himself would have been happy that the tiny creatures benefited from his daily spiritual gift. In fact Ma was sure he would. They had known each other for a brief time.

She took a deep breath and called his name. The statue's tiny eyes opened, glowing gold and green, the sign that a true deity was present.

Ma knelt down and touched his hand. "I will rip her to shreds," she thought, her mind racing angrily. "She will never rise again. How dare she strike the tiger?"

Hotei's voice drifted in the air around her. "Peace, old friend," he said. "Follow the path, and all that is evil will come undone of its own accord." He closed his eyes after that and was silent.

Ma knew he was right. She was allowing herself to become angry, a dangerous thing. Best to remain detached and focused. "What is going on with me," she thought.

She was over protective with David and not her usual calm thoughtful predator self. "If the Sorceress kills him, he will be back. Don't get too worked up." She knew even David wouldn't care if he died. All in a days work.

Ma got up and walked into the clinic. Detective Brenner and Winnie were waiting for her in the front room. "Winnie?" Ma asked, feigning surprise. "You are still here?"

"Just finishing some work when Detective Brenner arrived. Didn't want to leave him alone." Winnie's voice trailed off as she looked behind Dr. Ma for David. "Where's David?"

Winnie asked. Dr. Ma thought her tone was a bit sharp.

"Finishing up in the dojo," Ma answered, trying for a soothing tone.

"We thought we heard a scream," Jeremy offered. "I was going to check it out when Winnie headed me off and forced me to wait patiently for you two to finish your war games."

"War games indeed," Ma thought grimly. Aloud she said, "I didn't know you possessed any patience."

"I don't," Brenner said grinning. "That is one of my charms.

Look, Dr. Ma, we have the boat and the Captains body recovered. We also found one of the crew member's body's, but not a match to the DNA of the blood on the deck, floating further down the Intracoastal from the marina on the island.

Killer must have done him on the deck and tossed him overboard."

"Any leads on the killer?" Ma asked, not expecting any.

"DNA that doesn't belong to either victim," Brenner answered, surprising her. "We have a hit in the system, criminal past for assault and battery, out of Miami."

"Now we know who was the snack," Ma thought. Not the crew member after all. The Sorceress was pulling out all the stops this time. Only she could have been pulling strings in South Africa to go after David, having just orchestrated the Palm Beach boat caper.

Winnie suddenly darted towards the hallway. She met David halfway and started clucking and pecking at him like a mother hen.

He really did look terrible Ma thought. Pale face, normally pressed Brooks Brothers shirt and pants a bit rumpled, unsteady on his feet. Winnie was half dragging him into a chair while giving Dr. Ma a dirty sideways look.

"Whoa, bud," Brenner said with a whistle, "You look like shit. Dr. Ma hand you your ass?"

David gave him a wan smile. "Yep," he agreed, "Sometimes she overdoes it." He was being as truthful as possible. David was a terrible liar, so, he always told the truth.

"I didn't hurt him Winnie," Ma said to her assistant.

Winnie had shoved a cup of hot tea in David's hands before returning with a couple of his ever handy raw snack bars. "Eat," she said, handing them to him. It wasn't a question with Winnie. "I know you two skipped lunch."

"Dinner on us Jeremy?" Dr. Ma said, looking at Detective Brenner and sighing. "Let's catch up as a group on the case. Joy's doesn't deliver for dinner, I'll go pick it up. Winnie?"

"I have to get home," Winnie replied, still giving Dr. Ma her version of the stink eye for what she thought was Dr. Ma hurting David. "Get Detective Brenner his favorite ribs but make sure he doesn't leave a mess."

Brenner laughed. "Winnie," he said, "I wouldn't dare leave you a mess."

"Keep that in mind," Winnie called over her shoulder as she walked down the hall to the back door.

"I'll be right back," Ma said, following her down the hall.

After hearing the door closed, Detective Brenner looked at David and said "I have to talk with you about something."

Chapter Seven - The Case Unfolds

"Before Ma gets back," Brenner began, looking uncomfortable. "I am sorry about the situation with Karen. Ma told me on the phone that you and she might have had something going in South Africa.

She mentioned you two were coming by to check on the McCarthy's yesterday morning, when, ah, I was leaving."

David remained quiet, letting Brenner talk. The cop looked so uncomfortable, that David felt sorry for him. It wasn't Jeremy's fault that Karen had changed her mind about a relationship with David.

There was no blame to be passed around at all. "Just the Universal Plan," David thought, unhappily.

Not getting any answer, the detective pushed on. "We, Karen and I, dated a few times last year," he said. "Her parents were not happy about her dating a cop of all people so, we just let it go.

When I broke the news about her father, she asked me to stay overnight and watch the house personally. Nothing happened, we just talked, but I asked her out again and she agreed. She didn't mention you David. I'm sorry. I wouldn't have gone there. You know that."

The whole confession came out in a rush of words.

David just watched him carefully, expressionless and without comment until he was done. "No worries, Jeremy," David replied, finally. "She can make her own choice, and you are a great choice. Better than me by a long shot."

"I don't know," Jeremy said. "Her father would approve of you over me. Anyone like you over someone like me."

"Because of money?" David said.

"Yes," Jeremy replied. "No offense, but that seems to be important to Joseph."

"I'm sure it is," David said softly. "When we find him, I will tell him you are a good guy. We seem to have struck up some sort of friendship before the South Africa trip."

"Karen told me about that mess," Brenner said, his face clouding over angrily. "Thank god you were there."

"Joseph asked me to go with her," David replied. "I'm glad I went, but, it didn't save her from the trauma of what she witnessed." David was gently prying to see what Karen may may told Brenner.

"She seems to be handling it okay," the detective answered. "Her father being missing seems to have taken her mind off what happened."

David stayed silent, letting Brenner think for a moment.

"She said there was a big tiger," Brenner continued. "Some kind of genetic mutation by its colors, that must have been attracted to the campsite. She said it attacked everyone but you two and a few porters that got away."

"Weird thing though, she doesn't understand why a tiger would attack with all the gunfire. What do you remember, David?"

David realized that Jeremy had turned the interrogation technique back on him to get further information. "Well done," he thought. Aloud, he said, "I remember gunfire from our guys and from the bad guys and I grabbed Karen and ran. I don't remember seeing a tiger," he finished truthfully.

There would have to have been a large mirror available to do that.

Dr. Ma walked in carrying takeout from Joy's Happy Noodle Restaurant. "Hungry?" she asked. She could tell she interrupted a deep conversation. She would have to ask David later about it. At least he was not as pale now as he was right after her 'healing' session.

Following Dr. Ma's lead on eating before talking to benefit your digestion, the three polished off the Thai food in silence.

Jeremy had his usual sauce slathered ribs and fried dumplings washed down with a sugary soda.

David almost inhaled a massive helping of raw sliced vegetables that Joy tossed with spices and vinegar just for him.

Dr. Ma ate a light steamed vegetable and rice dish. The food was always delicious and fresh.

Taking a sip of the ginger and green tea she made at the well stocked tea bar in their waiting area, Ma began the discussion.

"Well, Jeremy, what news do you have about Joseph's disappearance?"

"The lab results from what we took off the boat showed the blood belonging to a known criminal out of Miami," Brenner began. "Miami Metro PD is looking for him as we speak.

Apparently, he was last seen a week ago in a convenience store surveillance camera, buying Lotto tickets."

"Interesting," Dr. Ma said.

"Very," Brenner added. "He let it be known that he and a friend were doing a job in Palm Beach for some rich guy. He was bragging about the money he was making."

"Joseph?" Ma asked.

"Possible," Brenner answered. "The blood came back to the bragging bad guy but nothing was found for the friend that may have come with him."

"Did you recover the body?" Ma asked. David looked up interestedly. He had been involved in this discovery when Ma partly opened the Spirit Wind sphere Maia had made.

"Not the match to the DNA," Brenner answered. "Looks like the Captain shot one crew member, and probably pushed him overboard. He was found floating south of where the boat was docked at the Marina in the Intracoastal Waterway.

"We also found what was probably a second crew member. Based on the surveillance cameras around the Marina, he left before getting onto the boat. He left kind of suddenly. Like something spooked him."

"His car was found on the north end of the island, abandoned. We don't know what killed him exactly. He was pushed or carried into the Intracoastal Waterway at some point."

"The body drifted and snagged in some coastline roots and rocks just before the end of Palm Beach Island."

"So, it was soon after the boat left from the Marina? Was the car up by North Lake Way and Lake Trail where it cuts through the rock there?" David asked. He looked at Dr. Ma. They both knew that place held some powerful and ancient magic.

"North of it actually. He was killed pretty soon after the cameras saw him leave the Marina," Brenner confirmed. "Silencer used for the crew member killed on the boat. Nobody in the area would have heard the shot.

Odd that nobody noticed the body floating around."

"Okay, Jeremy, I am going to give you some information that I can't exactly explain," Dr. Ma said carefully. Detective Brenner just looked at her, eyebrows raised. He was used to this kind of information from Dr. Ma and David by now.

"Shoot," Brenner said with a smile. "Better than me chasing my tail."

"First," Ma said, "you are never going to find the bragging bad guy from Miami's body. You can let them look, but don't expect it."

Brenner nodded. His every present paper notepad was out and he was scribbling away. Ma sighed, she hoped he would catch up with current electronics before he retired.

"Second," she continued, "The bragging guy's friend is alive and I think he is with Joseph."

Brenner's head snapped up and he looked at her with an open mouth. Quickly recovering himself, he looked down and kept writing.

"Seriously?" David interjected.

Ma hadn't shared this yet with David. She had seen it in the sphere and wanted to know how much his abilities had grown. Not as far as fine detail apparently.

"Yes," she confirmed. "He will contact everyone when he feels it is safe to do so. I don't know all the details, and I don't care really, but he won't be missing for long."

"At least I don't have another body to process," Brenner sighed. "Is that all?"

"One more thing," Ma said.

"Hit me with it," Brenner said, pen poised over his small pad.

"I wouldn't get too attached to the girl," Ma said, surprising both Jeremy and David. Dr. Ma almost never made any type of personal comments and observations that weren't absolutely necessary.

"Seriously?" David said again.

"What he just said," Brenner echoed.

"Just a hunch," Ma said. She stood up, picking up the take out containers. "Well boys, lets get going, its late."

Brenner snapped his notebook shut without another word. He was supposed to go to the McCarthy's after he finished with Dr. Ma. Karen wanted him to spend the night again. He would take Dr. Ma's warning with a grain of salt.

"Let me take that with me, Dr. Ma," Brenner said, taking the bag of empty take out containers from her. "Winnie will throw a fit tomorrow if there is any leftover food smell in her clinic."

"Thank you, Jeremy," Ma answered. "You know she would."

"Thanks for dinner as well," he said. Dr. Ma nodded and David locked the door after he left.

They both walked slowly down the hall, deep in thought. David paused as he was entering the code for the alarm.

They had a regular alarm system for the business. Winnie and the ancillary staff would not be able to open and close a ward like each had on their residences.

"What was the Karen warning about?" David asked Ma.

"Simply that she will find out you and Jeremy are friends, and that will cause her some problems," Ma said.

David just looked at her, waiting for more information. When none came from the reticent dragon, he asked. "Problems?"

"Come on David," Ma said, leaning past him to push the buttons for the alarm. They walked out and locked the back door. "She knows that the South Africa situation was not normal, and she distanced herself from you so she wouldn't have to think about it."

"And just fell back into Brenner's arms?" David said.

"Exactly so," Ma answered. "She is a hanger on. Her father has always taken care of her and he is missing. Her mother is no support to her. Jeremy is the epitome of big, strong, safe and stable. She liked him for that before, but Joseph wasn't going for the cop son in law thing."

"I wish I didn't see where you are going with this, but you are always dead on when it comes to reading people," David said.

"I wish I wasn't so *dead on* in this case, David," Ma said. "I think I need to take a look at her memories of South Africa, to make sure nothing will come back to bite us."

They were in her Mars red, Mercedes C63 AMG Coupe, driving to Palm Beach.

"Tonight?" David said, noting her route.

"Oh, no," Ma said smiling grimly. "First we check on your apartment. I don't trust Circe. She seems to have a new set of skills this time around. Then we go back to my place where I can keep an eye on you."

"I'm fine," David protested. He would be fine, that was true, but right now he was exhausted. He shouldn't have waited so long to show Ma the bruise. "What are you doing with the chunk you ripped out of me so nicely? The one you flash froze?"

"Hmm," Ma said, looking at him sideways. "You would prefer to keep it inside?"

"No," David said quickly. "I am just asking. I heard you say something about Bloodroot, right before I passed out for a moment. She poisoned me?" Ma nodded.

She parked in the street by Renato's back entrance and they walked up to his apartment door. Touching the rune lightly, they both entered the silent space. Too silent.

David moved right, crouching just out of the light that streamed in the long windows full of orchids. Ma moved left, mirroring his movements.

They couldn't easily transform in the small room without doing damage.

The orchids started whispering after a moment, greeting David and telling him that the ancient djinn had left earlier that day. She still hadn't returned. A visitor had come by the apartment and was trying to bypass the security rune.

Whoever or whatever had not been successful and had gone away. The djinn had left soon after.

David calmed the plants, misting them with his special water and food mixture. Soon, their voices were quiet.

Ma had been looking over the security rune for clues to the visitor's identity. "Clean," she said to David. "No damage and nothing left behind but an image that someone tried to tamper with it."

"Some*one*?" David asked.

"No, *something*," came a gritty, unused voice from the plant area behind him.

David spun around as Ma rushed into the apartment, securing the front door. "Nidi?

The ancient djinn was standing by the plants as if she had materialized from thin air. Which she might have if she could anymore. The energy for such a feat was a bit much for the old creature.

David was on her in a flash, fussing and looking her over for any signs of injury. "Are you all right?" he said, his voice full of concern.

Dr. Ma shook her head. It absolutely amazed her how attached David was to this crotchety old girl. She made a mental note, *again*, to ask him about their relationship. She always seemed to forget to do so.

After a millennia of forgetting to delve deeper into this situation it seemed necessary now. "No time like the present," Ma thought.

Dr. Ma strode up to the ancient djinn and placed a hand on the back of her neck. The little creature stiffened and went very still. David reached for Nidi angrily, saying, "No, don't do that, she is fragile."

David meant for Ma not to delve into the creature's mind by force, but Ma wasn't in the mood to back off.

She had been stressed since David's attack in South Africa and she was going to make sure this djinn, who she had always been suspicious of, was legit.

"Back off, David," Ma warned. Her skin started to change, melding with her long back hair into the finely scaled skin of her dragon. It wasn't a full transformation, just a backup to her warning.

David growled at her. Dr. Ma saw the same shimmer of partial transformation in him. She stopped what she was doing and looked at him in surprise.

"You *dare*," she said, angrily, her voice hissing with a slight dragon quality. "I will rip you apart where you stand, boy."

David returned to his full human guise, even if he was still growling. He knew better than to push the dragon too far. She had been a bit on the edge lately.

"Let her go," he said quietly. "I will tell you what you need to know about her, but don't hurt her. Your little mental 'explorations' are not painless."

Ma watched him for a moment and then let the djinn go. The creature collapsed as she released her grip, but David snatched her up before she hit the floor.

He sat on the highly polished wood and held her to him like a rag doll, glaring at Ma.

"She would have tried to protect me, that is all. She came from Kaia," he said, naming a legendary immortal.

Now it was Ma's turn to be surprised. She sat next to him and said, "I'm sorry, I didn't know."

"I should have told you long ago," David said apologetically. "I just figured you would probably insist on retiring her if you knew her real age."

"As well I should," Ma replied, still staring at him in surprise. "She can live at the Library for now. David, this is serious. Circe is a serious threat."

Nidi mumbled something and opened her eyes. She took in David, holding her in his arms and sighed. "Great Tiger," she greeted him.

"Faithful servant," he greeted her back with respect. "What happened here? Where did you go and why did you not call to me?"

The Elementals' djinn were linked to them, mentally, if the situation warranted it. Kind of like an alarm company calling your cell phone to report your house alarm was going off. But better. Nidi, if capable, could have alerted David easily by just calling for him in her mind.

"I did not wish to disturb you for something so small," Nidi replied, very softly. David had to bend his head close to her to hear her in his human guise. "The one who would kill you was not here, just their scout."

Ma's lips pressed together tightly at Nidi's words. "That's it," she said to David. "We are leaving right now. Nidi will recover better in the Library."

"You take her," David said to Dr. Ma. "Let me just settle things here. I have an auto watering system I have been meaning to try out for the orchids. I just want to set up remote surveillance system for your house to ensure the watering system works."

Ma frowned. "I will see you later then," she said, less than happily. She took the again unconscious djinn from David and walked to his front door.

Humans would just see her carrying what looked like an antique doll out to her car on the curb. The djinn did not appear to be a living thing, although she was. Well, define living! Besides, it was dark out and Peruvian was not well lit where she had parked.

"I may stay the night here," David said slowly, expecting Ma to object.

"No!" she said immediately.

"Yes," David said quietly but firmly. " I want to see what comes back, if anything. I am perfectly capable of taking care of myself and you know it."

"No I do not know that," Dr. Ma said. "Fine, be stubborn. Stay here tonight if you wish, but take precautions. Do you want me to send Mort?"

David laughed. "Yeah, no," he said. "Mort really does not like me much, and I will be fine."

"You had better be fine," Ma said, walking out with the unconscious djinn and securing David's front door with the security rune.

She knew that David was becoming anxious, being around her so much lately. "He thinks I don't know how feels around me," she thought. "Worse, he thinks I am not affected by him either."

Dr. Ma placed the ancient djinn in the front seat next to her and seat belted her in. Or tried to. "I should have brought a child's seat," Ma thought gloomily. She made the 10 minute drive to her residence in half that.

Unbuckling the still unresponsive djinn, she lifted her and walked to the front door. Releasing her own security rune, she walked into her home.

Passing through the center great room and out the glass window/doors that framed her beautifully over grown garden, she paused at the stone fountain.

Berenice opened her eyes before Ma touched her and briefly said, "I heard," before Ma dipped her fingers to the softly tinkling water. In a split second, they were both standing in the library. Maia walked up to greet Dr. Ma, a perplexed look on her face.

"What is going on lately?" Maia asked. "Its like Grand Central Station in here. Now you have Kaia's djinn for me to take care of?" The lovely Spirit woman took the unresponsive djinn from Ma's arms.

Ma stared at her. "What?" Maia said. "I may be mostly ether, but I am capable of enough energy expression to carry a djinn!"

"No," Ma said, surprised. "How did you know Nidi was Kaia's djinn?

"Please," Maia said turning and walking away with the little creature. "Who didn't know she gave her to David? She has lots anyway."

"Who didn't know?" Ma said under her breath. "I didn't know for one."

"I heard that," Maia called over her shoulder as she walked away with Nidi in her arms. "You and the tiger should get to know each other better." She turned and flashed a smile at Ma as she disappeared through a wall.

"As if we could," Ma said. She turned to Berenice. "Time to go. I need to make a few calls before this evening gets any more interesting." She dipped her hand in Berenice's fountain and they were back in Ma's garden.

"Thank you," Ma called, not looking back as she headed into her house.

Berenice said loudly, to make sure Ma heard, "Do you want me to check on David at his place?"

"No, thank you," Ma replied. "We need you just where you are."

Berenice pouted slightly. "Party pooper," she said glumly. "It's not as if you really need me to get in there."

"I heard that," came from Dr. Ma inside the house.

Mort was waiting for her. "Do I smell ancient djinn?" He would have plenty of trace scent available on the air after Dr. Ma carried Nidi through the house.

"Well who else," Ma almost snapped. "I suppose even you knew Nidi was a gift from Kaia to David?"

"Well who didn't?" Mort responded and then dematerialized.

"Me!" Ma said to thin air. She picked up the her cell phone and touched Jeremy Brenner's picture under her 'Favorites.' When he didn't answer, she left a message. "Jeremy, its Dr.

Ma. Meet me for coffee at the clinic early. Better yet, take the morning class. We will have coffee afterwards in my office."

Ma decided to start her rest period early tonight. She hadn't slept in centuries or longer. As many hours as she could manage in a deep delta state of meditation, lying in her bed, was enough to restore and maintain her human body.

She stripped off her clothing from the day and stepped into an already steaming shower of filtered saline water.

Ma used a special filtering system in her residence that removed all impurities and chemicals from her water and then added what she needed.

Her shower added a sea salt infusion for a healthful steam of her lungs and scrub of her body. She could use mint or other herbal oils at will from a specially designed pump.

David loved the shower in his guest suite at her house. The old plumbing in his apartment didn't allowed for much modification. She had had a custom deep soaking tub installed in his Palm

Beach digs. The saline and herbal infusions there came from an attachment to the tub.

The rest of Ma's house used a high alkaline system to drink, brush your teeth or cook. She even had the by product acid waste water, diverted to her massive garden. The plants loved the acid water.

She slipped naked between her 800 thread count, satin weave Egyptian organic cotton sheets and closed her eyes, sighing. There was plenty to process but she needed to shelve it all to recoup.

Tomorrow would be here soon enough.

Chapter Eight - Jeremy and Gracie

Detective Brenner received Dr. Ma's message a couple of hours later and set his alarm to get up early enough to make the morning martial arts class at the Mugen Dojo.

He had been following up on leads and reports from the cases all day. He still had the disappearance of Joseph McCarthy as a priority.

Ma had reassured him that Joseph was fine and would be home soon. The problem was he couldn't tell anybody. Oh, he could, but that might come with a psych eval when he said he just 'knew' it, he could not 'prove' it.

He felt sorry for Ann McCarthy, she was starting to look like a shell of her former self. Ann had made plans to travel to their Summer home in Sag Harbor next week.

She was trying to get Karen to go with her, but her daughter was stubborn. Somehow she had convinced herself that waiting for her father's return in their Palm Beach home would be better.

It was the last place her father had been seen by the family.

Ann asked Jeremy to intervene, but the conversation had not gone particularly well. Karen was happy with the arrangement she had with the detective staying at their house every night. She said she would stay in Palm Beach and monitor the investigation through Brenner.

Jeremy himself was not sure he was as happy as Karen with their nightly sleep over arrangements. He hadn't been back to his apartment in West Palm Beach except for one time to pack some clothing.

He didn't need much to stay with Karen. They had every amenity a guest could want, including laundering his clothing and sending his suits to the dry cleaner.

Jeremy also felt uncomfortable around Ann McCarthy now that he was sleeping with her daughter every night at their house. Karen had her own suite, but you still saw the other residents of the large home in passing.

He also had to interact with Ann regarding her husband's disappearance.

She stopped him heading up the left side staircase late last night. "Before you make my daughter's night, again," she said to him, dryly. "Tell me what more you know about my husband's whereabouts."

Wanting to relieve the woman's anxiety, and his own by getting away from her, he told her that Dr. Ma felt that Joseph was close to being found.

"I know there is no evidence to support this," he said, looking at her in the dim light of the entrance hall. "But I know Dr. Ma well, she is usually right."

He couldn't believe he had just said that to her. Police investigations didn't base their statements to family members on psychic type hunches. Ann seemed to take his statement well.

"I feel the same way," she said. "He isn't dead. I would know it." Looking at him thoughtfully, she said, "Well, enjoy your night," and walked away up the right side staircase.

Detective Brenner continued up to Karen's suite. He was hoping she might be asleep, it was late. At least for him. He kept forgetting, she slept in every morning and then lived her leisurely lifestyle as she wished. She didn't have a job. She didn't have to clean the house, or go grocery shopping. She could take a nap in the middle of the day.

Jeremy slipped into Karen's bed and she immediately reached for him. She pressed her lips against his and rolled over on top of him. Her warm, naked body stretched the length of his, pressing against him invitingly. "You're late," she said softly kissing his face and neck. "Any news about Dad?"

Jeremy ran his hands down her firm back and buttocks. Tennis and a private trainer kept her in shape. She was slim and toned, not to mention beautiful. Her black hair and blue eyes stood out from creamy white skin. She had her father's coloration.

Jeremy wasn't purely Irish like Karen, his family was English, Scottish and Irish. The Irish had won out in his small section of the family and influenced the way he was raised as a child.

"Not really," Jeremy answered, kissing her back. "I told your mother that Dr. Ma has a feeling we will find him soon, but, I have absolutely nothing concrete to go on."

He had stopped their foreplay while answering her about her father's case. His eyes had that distant look they get when his mind gets wrapped up in his case details.

Karen brought his mind back to her and sex by slipping her hand down his abdomen under the covers. His eyes snapped back to her and he bit his lip to stop from groaning out loud. "That's a good boy," she said, continuing to let her hands explore his hard, muscled body.

She seemed especially interested in the scar he had from being shot on duty. It was still sensitive after all this time. She made sure to use that to her advantage.

"Karen," Jeremy said, pulling her closer to him and looking at her intently. "What are we doing here?"

"What do you mean?" Karen asked him, feigning innocence.

"Us, here," Jeremy pressed on, not wanting to lose momentum. " I get the impression your mother thinks I am a passing thing for you. Sometimes I get the feeling that you think that as well." There, he had said it. He wasn't trying to rush things with her. The practical cop just wanted to know if an end game had already been planned for the second manifestation of the Jeremy and Karen show. She had dumped him before, after all.

"Jeremy," Karen answered, taking his face in her hands. " I am crazy about you. I should have never let you go before. Don't worry about my mother. I make my own decisions, and I want you."

Brenner was better than just a good cop. He was a great investigator. People lied to him all day long. He didn't believe her for a minute. He could easily get her to tell him the truth, but, who wanted the truth when a beautiful, warm and naked young woman was half wrapped around you?

Definitely not him. At least right now. He would worry about the future later.

After a night with Karen, who was always full of sexual energy, he may not do very well in class tomorrow. He wasn't sure how long this thing with her would or should last, but he would enjoy being with Karen tonight.
He had a momentary guilty thought about David. He knew he was lied to when David said

there wasn't anything much going on with him and Karen.

Every woman and man Jeremy had ever met seemed to be interested in David. He tried hard to remember who David had been interested in. Not many.

Karen was sleeping soundly when he got up the next morning. He quickly showered, shaved and dressed, trying not to wake her. It wasn't likely he would, unless he accidentally fired his gun while placing it in his shoulder holster. She slept like the dead, snoring softly.

Grabbing a cup of coffee and danish from the early morning tray one of the McCarthy servants had left (they were beginning to know his crazy hours) he hurried out the door in his dojo training gear.

Black coolmax sweat wicking t-shirts and a high tech stretch pant in similar material. Man's best friend, on over his Hanes for any potential hazards in class, and he was off.

The shoulder holster and badge clipped to his sweat pants was only for his time in the police issued car.

His dry cleaned and pressed suit and shirt were hung in the back of his police vehicle. One good thing about staying in Palm Beach overnight, you got to keep the unmarked police car in the Town limits.

Since he was meeting with Dr. Ma after class about the case, he could drive it there too. He was saving in gas and wear and tear on his POV (personally owned vehicle) and having sex every night.

It was hard to see a downside.

Parking his car in the shared lot behind Dr. Ma and David's Traditional Chinese Medical Clinic and their martial arts studio, the Mugen Dojo, Brenner hurried around to the front door.

He had been in and out of the back door many times, but it was expected for students to use the front door. Right now he was a student.

A pretty blond woman was entering the school as Brenner reached the front door. He recognized her from some of the classes. David had spoken about her having Olympic dreams or something.

"Gracie, right?" Brenner said as he held the door open for her.

The fit and graceful young woman gave a start when he used her name. "Yes," she said carefully. "Do we know each other?"

Brenner accepted the slight blow to his ego. She was at least ten years younger than him and very focused on her training. He was a hyper observant cop. There was no reason she would remember him, much less know his name like he knew hers.

He felt a bit like a stalker having called her by name. "Detective Jeremy Brenner," he said, hoping to put her at ease by knowing he was one of the good guys.

"Oh, yes," Gracie said. "Dr. David and Dr. Ma's cop friend. I am sorry, I, um, didn't recognize you." Gracie walked in ahead of Jeremy as he held the door for her.

"Didn't recognize me?" he thought. Lame. DIdn't bother to notice I existed, yes. Kids these days all had their heads buried in their cell phones. What was she, 18 years old?

Gracie walked away to the women's locker room quickly to hide her embarrassment. She actually had no problem recognizing the detective.

She had been startled when he called her by name. "I can't believe he knows my name," she had thought to herself. She had certainly noticed him.

Outside of her instructor David, Detective Brenner was the hottest guy in the martial arts school. Sandy ginger hair, close cropped in a typical cop like or military cut and light blue eyes in a freckled face made him appear younger than she was sure he was.

David was at the front of the school, finishing his own routine when Jeremy started stretching out in the place he usually sat for class.

David paused and said, "Are you here voluntarily?"

Brenner grinned. David knew he preferred night classes. The busy detective was always up late, working cases. Early morning classes were not his usual choice.

"Command performance," he said. "Joining you guys for coffee, and I hope, breakfast afterwards."

"First I am hearing of it," David said smiling. Gracie took a spot next to Detective Brenner and started her own warm up.

"Am I in your spot?" he said politely. Students who were regulars often had a favorite spot in the class. Someone as intense as Gracie probably stood right up front, next to the instructor.

"Nah," she said, not completely truthfully. He was in her favorite spot. "I'm fine here."

David listened to this whole exchange, smiling to himself. "Now that was a good match for Brenner," he thought. They were a lot alike, intense and no nonsense.

Better than Karen for his friend any day. He didn't think the age difference was a big deal, about ten years. But, what did ten years mean to someone who was over a thousand? He was at least a thousand years younger that Ma and he thought she was hot.

David looked up as Dr. Ma joined him at the front of the class.

Gracie and Jeremy Brenner looked up too, as did the rest of the dozen or so students. Everyone quickly settled into place, including David. He stood respectfully a stride behind her and next to her. 'This could only mean a mirroring lesson," he thought.

David looked at Gracie and Jeremy in front of him and smiled. They were about the same height, this should be interesting.

Dr. Ma bowed slightly to the class and then to David. All returned her bow but deeper, with great respect. She didn't utter a word as she faced the class and began demonstrating the form.

David followed her lead in exactly the same sequence, mirroring her every movement, even the subtle ones, without a single error.

The students, even those who had seen this before, were entranced. The mirrored movements were graceful and beautiful and somewhat terrifying in their precise, gravity defying quality.

The two masters, David and Ma, never once looked up or at each other. Their eyes were unfocused and their movements silent. You could barely hear a breath exhaled here and there.

For Gracie, she had never seen this demonstration. She was in awe. Brenner had seen this before, but it still had the same effect on him.

Dr. Ma stilled her movements as if she had never begun them. David stopped in tandem with her. You could hear a pin drop. It was deathly silent. Ma waved briefly at students, pairing them up. Brenner and Gracie were her first pairing.

Gracie looked at Brenner flushing slightly. She didn't know if she was going to be capable of this type of paired movement.

Jeremy slid his gaze sideways, indicating she should step behind him and to the side like David had with Dr. Ma. Not a sexist thing at all. He had done this before, so he would lead.

When all the students were arranged like she and David had been, Ma raised her voice to speak. The words flowed out into the silent room, wrapping gently around each student, slipping into the varied recesses of their brains.

"Lead student," Ma said. "Practice the form on me. I will face the same direction as you and you will move when I move." She changed her position in front of them.

"Mirror," she continued, her voice still seeming to come from everywhere despite her change of direction. "Un-focus your eyes and move when your lead moves. Breath when your lead breathes. Empty your mind of all thoughts."

David repositioned himself, but instead of stepping behind her, he stayed in front and to the side. His eyes were closed. Despite this, he started exactly on time with Ma's opening movement and stayed with her, flawlessly, the entire form.

When it was over, Gracie felt like she had run a marathon. She concentrated so hard, she thought she would burst. Dr. Ma and David faced the class, bowed and left by the back door.

Gracie turned to Jeremy Brenner only to find him following the instructors out of the back exit. They were all walking together chatting softly.

Jet Carlson, the assistant teaching student, was answering questions and getting ready to the close the school when everybody finished their excitement about the mirroring lesson.

Gracie watched Detective Brenner close the back door. "Nice guy, nicer butt," she thought. "Ugh, Gracie, all you think about is martial arts and the sexy guys in class." Well the sexy teacher and the sexy guy in class. "Grow up!" she told herself and she retrieved her gear and left.

She saw what looked like an undercover police car in the parking lot as she got into her little blue Jetta. Acting on impulse, she jotted a quick note to thank Jeremy for his help in class and tucked it under the windshield wiper of the car.

She looked around carefully. It was most likely his car. She recognized everyone else's rides. Except Dr. David. He ran everywhere.

"What are you doing?" she thought to herself as she got in her car to leave. A cop? Older than her? Ugh! She wondered what was wrong with her sometimes. Still, she left the note there and drove away.

Inside, Jeremy was sitting down to a hot cup of coffee and the fresh danish Winnie had left out for him. Dr. Ma had asked her to bring breakfast for Detective Brenner. She had brought an assortment of sugary danish.

Forget Karen and the cute young girl in the dojo this morning. Winnie was his kind of woman.

"Thank you Winnie," Brenner said around a mouthful of danish. Winnie shook her head, probably at him talking with his mouth full and walked back to her desk. A carefully selected fresh danish was perched on a napkin in her hand.

Brenner had taken a shower after David and quickly dressed in his suit and shirt. His sweaty training clothes were stuffed in the zip portion of his workout bag. They should be ripe when he took them out tonight after sitting in his car all day.

David appeared, perfectly attired in Brooks Brothers pants and a button down shirt. Both pants and shirt, were perfectly tailored to his lean muscular figure.

Detective Brenner was adapting to the strange feelings he had around David. It seemed the tall and stunning man was like a Pied Piper to anything breathing around him.

"If I am ever interested in men," Brenner thought, stuffing a second danish in his mouth with a big swig of coffee, "and it is not likely before hell freezes over, I hope it's someone as good looking as him."

He wiped crumbs off his chin. "Not, that *that* would ever happen in this lifetime," Brenner reassured himself.

David sat down after making himself a cup of tea at the well stocked tea bar the clinic waiting room provided.

He pulled out a pre-prepared baggie of dried fruit, nuts and seeds and sat down to enjoy his breakfast. Mostly raw vegan, he had a fast metabolism. The baggie would be just one of 7-8 mini meals he would consume today.

"Your know I hate early classes," Brenner said, "but, that mirror Tai Chi form things gets me every time. You two are just incredible."

David smiled at the compliment. "Not so hard to be a perfect pair after a millennia of practice," he thought. Aloud he said, "Thank you Jeremy. You and Gracie made a good team. You are a natural pair."

Brenner flushed slightly. David's words seemed to carry a certain connotation. David knew that Jeremy was still seeing Karen. Brenner was a one woman kind of guy. Even when it was the wrong woman. "What is she," he asked David, "Eighteen?"

"Twenty one," David answered. "You should get to know her better, come to class and train with her, she will be a famous Olympian one day."

Brenner looked at him, eyebrows coming together as he frowned slightly. Thank goodness Dr. Ma saved him from further comment. She breezed in with a cup of tea already in her hand.

Jeremy always appreciated that the two of them dressed so nicely for their day. It was a real sign of professionalism.

Dr. Ma had a crisp, white and perfectly fitted lab coat on over a Ponte knit J. McLaughlin sheath dress. A pair of Kate Spade mid level heels in shell pink complimented the ivory dress. An 18" strand of Mikimoto pearls, a soft ivory color set off the look.

"You look stunning Dr. Ma," Jeremy said. "I just saw you in training gear, your hair pulled back and here you are in no time looking like you just stepped out of Vogue magazine."

Dr. Ma laughed. "Are you flirting with me Jeremy Brenner?" she said smiling. "I am old enough to be your mother."

"No sensei," Jeremy said politely. "I am just being observant, like a good cop. Also, you definitely do not remind me of my mother."

"Okay, spill the beans on the investigation," David said. He was stealing admiring glances at Dr. Ma himself. She was way too old for Jeremy true, but what about him?

If Ma chose anybody on the earthly plane of existence, David would fight to make sure it was going to be him.

Too late, he shielded his thoughts. Ma had heard him loud and clear.

To her credit, she just looked him and raised her eyebrows slightly.

Chapter Nine - The Murders in Review

"Well." Detective Brenner began after two and a half danishes. He would finish the third, the blueberry one before he left to avoid spills in his undercover police car.

It was against policy to have food and drink in the cars, but everyone did it. You just couldn't get caught was all.

"We are starting to make some progress." Brenner took a few more swigs of coffee and continued. "We found the second man who came up from Miami. He says he stayed in the car and never saw the first guy again.

He also claims he dropped Joseph off at Lantana Private Airport at his request and never saw him again. I don't believe him, but we have a statement and his DNA."

Both David and Dr. Ma smiled and congratulated him at once. "If anyone can solve this mess," Ma said, "It will be you Jeremy."

"There is only so far you can go with what little we have," Brenner said glumly. "The first man is missing, and, if you are correct Dr. Ma, he will stay that way. The gun used to shoot him was recovered by divers off the island chain and proves the Captain offed him. Captain is dead, so case closed.

The Captain apparently died of some type of internal hemorrhage. They are short of calling it an aneurysm."

"What about the crew members found floating on the west side of Palm Beach Island?" David asked.

"SGW on the first one," Brenner said, meaning 'single gunshot wound.' "Also attributable to the Captain. It was the same gun and the residue on his hands seemed enough for more than one shot.

Another case closed. The second we still don't know what killed him."

"There must be quite a lot of furor on the Island over a body floating up uninvited," Dr. Ma teased the detective, smiling.

"Yes indeed," Brenner said with a sigh. "Half my job lately has been going house to house reassuring staff, then coming back and spending the afternoon on the phone reassuring the residents who have left for the Summer."

"Reassuring them what?" David said curiously.

Detective Brenner looked at him for a moment before replying. "It amazes me that you grew up in the same or, if I am to believe what Karen says, better circumstances financially than many of my residents."

"What is he talking about?" David said, looking at Dr. Ma for clarification.

"He is trying to say you are an anomaly, David," Dr. Ma smiled.

"Anomaly is short of what I was thinking," Brenner said, shaking his head. "David, you grew up wealthy, still have a ton of money, unless it is all Dr. Ma's," Brenner looked quizzically at her but she didn't answer.

She just grinned at David.

"So, I am your sugar mama?" she said looking at David and laughing. Brenner didn't know that David was her adopted son. That she was aware of. As great a detective as he was though, he could know, and just be holding the information close to the vest.

"Not really," David answered truthfully. " I have money of my own from my parents," he said to Jeremy shyly. David had always been uncomfortable about having so much money. It was impossible not to with their Elemental lives and jobs.

It was the difference between success and failure.

"You dress, live and definitely function below your financial stratosphere," Jeremy continued, talking about David. "I think I know you well enough to say you are just a regular guy in, well, many aspects. Our guys in uniform take the craziest calls for service from the residents."

"But that is the nature of the people who live on the Island," Dr. Ma said.

"Yes," Detective Brenner replied. "I am very happy working there, I love the uniqueness of our seasonal occupants. I just find David to be a fish out of water in a pond he may very well own without me knowing."

David flushed slightly. He had finally gotten the gist of what Brenner was saying. "Dr. Ma is not much different than I am. She lives in West Palm Beach and works for a living."

"Lets not stretch 'works for a living,' David," Ma laughed. "Jeremy is right, you are a bit of an innocent in a pond of barracudas."

Now it was Brenner's turn to laugh. "I've seen him negotiating social events when I was there at a detail. That is a fair description. Look guys, I have to fly, tons of work left to do." He turned to Dr. Ma, "When will I be able to close this missing persons case?"

"Give it a day or two and you should be free of that burden," Ma replied cryptically.
"Good enough," Detective Brenner said and left.

Winnie came in the front door while Jeremy was heading out. Brenner gave her a quick peck on the cheek and thanked her for breakfast. She smiled at him and locked the front door.

It wasn't quite time for patients and Winnie tolerated no interruptions to her routine. The three of them were lucky she didn't make them sit outside for their little breakfast meeting.

Dr. Ma watched the interaction between Winnie and Detective Brenner. He didn't receive the usual swat from his affectionate peck on the cheek that David did. Winnie was either softening up, or she felt differently about the two men.

Ma decided she would keep an eye on this situation. Winnie's instincts were usually spot on.

"Detective Brenner said I could take a trip to the morgue to see the bodies and tour Joseph's boat at the dock," Dr. Ma said to David.

"When did he say that?" David looked up from his perusal of their waiting area's tea bar. "We need to order more Sencha." The slightly bitter pale green tea was a favorite of his.

"When I spoke with him by phone," Ma answered. "I forgot to mention it to him today. We have a light afternoon if you can handle the patient load, I will get at least one or both visits handled."

"I'm fine," David replied. "Winnie?"

"You can certainly handle it," Winnie sniffed, looking a bit hard at Dr. Ma. "I will chaperone. A few of Dr. David's fans are coming in and they behave much better when Dr. Ma is here."

Ma laughed aloud. "Why Winnie," she said, "You are much more scary than I am when you want to be."

"I am just here to keep the appointments flowing," Winnie said with a slight frown. "I would rather not have to go into the exam rooms, but I will."

"Ladies," David interrupted, "I can handle things myself."
Now both Winnie and Ma laughed. "Right," Winnie said, waving him off. "Don't worry Dr. Ma," she said. "I will handle things."

Dr. Ma had Winnie call Detective Brenner to say she would be stopping by the morgue when he told her the bodies would be available. Then she would go to Joseph's boat. The detective made arrangements to meet her after lunch, about 1:30 PM.

The morning brought a dozen patients for Dr. Ma and David. Triathlon season was ramping up and so were the injuries their other sport patients seemed to incur while trying to enjoy late Spring and Summer activities.

Dr. Ma had a world class female tennis player with a serious muscle tear from trying to play catch football in her backyard. She winced when she saw the spectacular swelling and bruising over and around the woman's right thumb.

"You are right handed?" she asked her patient, already knowing the answer was yes.

"Yes," the player said in her charming Dutch accent. Dr. Ma smiled. She really liked this patient. She and her husband lived a very healthy lifestyle that would keep them both fit and functional for the rest over their lives. Some athletes struggle after they stop competing, but she was sure this one would thrive.

"So," Dr. Ma said, "Your coach should be having a minor heart attack right now. Didn't you get the wildcard spot at Wimbledon?" The woman nodded affirmatively.

"No time to waste then," Ma said.

"This is going to hurt," the tennis champion said, making a face.

"Yep," Dr. Ma responded, "But you are tough. We will get through this and you will play well."

Needling, cupping, manipulating and injecting, made up the lengthy and complex first treatment. Qigong was woven into the tapestry of the treatment.

Manipulation of Qi, or what the Chinese refer to as 'energy,' was not difficult for an Elemental. Being comprised of elemental energies made you rather knowledgable about how they worked.

Dr. Ma could heal fractures at a greatly accelerated pace, help shrink tumors, encourage soft tissue tears to repair and many other things with energy. But, it was not that simple from the patient's standpoint. Not everyone participates the same.

The tennis player left smiling. Her thumb injury actually felt much better. She knew she had several treatments ahead of her though. She had come to Dr. Ma for torn abdominal muscles, rehab for a spinal injury and much more.

She always said that nobody in their right mind would seek treatment with Dr. Ma if they didn't have a serious goal.

Ma wished she was right. She never did well with non goal oriented patients. She gave those to David to coddle and care for.

Several case followups filled most of the morning. Everyone was doing well, so Dr. Ma chalked this up as a good day.

Meanwhile, David was having his own patient case issues. He usually took the complex cases, involving internal medicine or long term injury rehabilitation. Dr. Ma took the rapid resolution, external medical applications.

He would take the muscle disease case and she would take the muscle injury case. He was the king of compassion and patience as his patients healed.

Dr. Ma was known to tell her athletic injury patients to suck it up and get back in training. A little pain never hurt anyone. Together in the same practice, they were the perfect balance.

Chapter Ten - A Trip To The Morgue

Leaving after a quick lunch of leftovers with David, Dr. Ma got into her Mercedes and headed towards the Palm Beach County Medical Examiner's office.

She had decided that morning she needed wrap up the details of Circe's crimes against humans before taking her out. She was also concerned they had missed something the Sorceress had created to do her bidding on the earthly plane.

"What *exactly* had happened in South Africa?" Ma mused. There were ways of finding out the details. She had exhausted several of them already. Information in the Library was often missing finer details.

It was something like a good mystery writer leaving out the very thing that the reader wanted to know.

The story written in the Akashic records seemed complete, unless you needed to examine a detail minutely. For that, you often had to visit the location, touch the object or in

Ma's case, dig into the minds and memories or those involved.

You may have had a latte this morning with a croissant at your favorite Starbucks. You may go there every day. The staff may know your name.

Now, try remembering the name and phone number on the bottom of the poster that hangs directly above the utensil and napkin area. You have seen it there hundreds of times.

If the name and number meant the difference between you getting a million dollars tax free or not, you would go back the storefront and get that number!

Dr. Ma chose the visit to the morgue first. Detective Brenner met her there, all business in front of colleagues and co-workers.

"Dr. Ma, how are you today?" he greeted her, holding out his hand to deliver a firm handshake. "Please come with me." He led the way to the area of cold storage vaults that held the bodies from this case.

She suppressed a smile as they walked past offices and exam rooms. Visitors always attracted curiosity here. Nobody normal just came for fun. It was always business. Some people wouldn't even come when it was business.

Some folks were sensitive enough to feel the energy coming off the deceased bodies. Energy detailing the methods of their demise.

The energy didn't bother Dr. Ma. To her, the leftover fields of expression were like a series of holograms. Each was projected over, under, or around the deceased. Each played the same clip again and again. It wasn't as if there was anybody home. It was merely a film clip.

Even the Spirit Winds that visited Dr. Ma weren't *thinking* in a present sense sort of way.

They were very realistic mini documentaries. Narrated by the victim, to be sure. Gave them a rather serious tinge of reality, but they were still past tense.

Ma remembered going to the movies with David to see a famous film, based on a famous book, something about witches and wizards. Big attraction in Disney World right now. One of the actors said something to the effect of watching out for things that could think, especially if you couldn't see where they kept their brain.

She and David had laughed at that comment. It was so true! They wondered if the writer was an Otherworldly herself. Both had enjoyed the movie and promised to see the next one. They hadn't delivered on that promise yet and it was years ago.

Time flies when you are having fun.

The character in the movie was right. When something that was not an Otherworldly entity could think, well now you have something to be worried about. Dead human bodies, inanimate objects and so forth.

Cognition was about a big 'tell.' Otherworldly entities also had those lapis blue eyes. If you noticed such things. I guess they could always wear contacts to conceal the distinct color, but red eyes for instance were never good.

Dr. Ma was only looking for holograms today, at best, a mini documentary clip. She came prepared. The sphere from Maia was in her handbag as well as the frozen (not cold frozen but flash frozen to desiccation) bit of tissue and poison from David.

The objects would know their kin and be drawn to them. She even had a scrap of fabric, blood soaked, from her original exploration of Joseph's boat.

She didn't feel badly, depriving the Crime Scene Units of this bit of evidence. They had a large smear of blood to work with on the deck. Other bits of fabric were stuck to the big dried blood smear. Hers was just one of many.

The bit of flesh that she had recovered from the boat Captain was not there. She had gotten all she needed from Allistair when he swallowed and 'read' it for her in the Library.

Besides, the Captain's decomposing body was recovered from the boat and lie in repose in one of these very stainless steel storage areas.

Dr. Ma didn't know how to explain to anyone that the advanced level of decomposition was due to two mitigating factors. The first, was that he had died prior to even taking off from the Palm Beach marina location.

The second would have been even harder to express in medical terms.

When you rip the soul or essence out of a living being, it deteriorates rapidly. Hence the myth that was not at all a myth, about zombies. Human bodies didn't decompose at the rate the zombies' bodies decomposed.

They were soul deprived dead folks. Human essence was bound to their tissue and tearing the two apart accelerated the decomposition of their physical body.

She and David had also watched one of those zombie movies once. Leaving the theater, they had both been surprised at how many people seemed to want the zombie manifestation to be real. 'Cool' and other words were being used to describe how the people would feel when they met a zombie.

"Well," Ma had noted to David. "They definitely aren't 'cool,' they are warm from decomposition and, they smell awful. Why would they want to see one?"

"They want to see it because they don't think they ever will," David had replied. "They don't believe zombies are real."

"Why is the truth harder to believe than fiction?" Dr. Ma said, shaking her head.

"Look at the Judeo Christian beliefs," David commented. "You can do just about anything in front of humans and after awhile they will just say, not real, just a story."

"Agreed," Ma had said. " I really like the whole raising the dead thing Jesus Christ did though, didn't you?"

"Way better than the zombie thing," David agreed. "Animating a corpse is nothing on the guy that regenerated the whole thing into a living organism. Now that *is* some stuff."

Dr. Ma was smiling at her recollections as the Medical Examiner pulled the three bodies from their refrigeration compartments. The other doctor looked at her oddly. Perhaps it was her smile.

"Sorry," Dr. Ma said, "I was thinking about something else. Thank you for your help."

"No problem," the M.E. replied. "If you need anything I will be next door catching up on some paperwork. My assistant will stay with you to make sure the bodies are properly, ah, put away."

Dr. Ma knew the M.E. was suspicious of her request to see the bodies and didn't want to leave her alone with them.

Detective Brenner was sitting in the hall outside, scribbling notes in his ever present pocket pad while talking on his cell phone. He always said that seeing bodies once, if needed, was all he wanted to do.

Any more and he would have gone to medical school and studied forensics.

Dr. Ma smiled at the assistant as the M.E. left the room. "Thank you so much for staying. I don't have to see many dead bodies in my field. Although I like helping the police in their investigations, it can get a bit creepy, don't you think?"

Her monotone manner of speaking, almost hypnotic, lulled the young man enough for him to approach her, standing next to the boat Captains body on his sliding stainless steel tray.

He reached out a hand to pat her arm, reassuring her. "Perfect," Ma thought as she slipped her own hand over his.

A slightly glazed expression came over the assistants face. "You are going to be so helpful," Ma said, drawing his memories out into the space between him and her.

Manipulating the slivery glowing threads she wound around the small army of pictures from the assistant's mind, she reworked what he would remember. About today. Helping her with the bodies that was.

When she was done, she tucked the silver thread woven, thought pictures back into the young man's head and went to work.

First, Ma pulled out the frozen bit of David's flesh wrapped around the Bloodroot poison. Holding it in her hand, she stood over each body in turn.

No reaction from any of them in their respective aural presences. Aura was simply bioelectrical or biochemical signature expressed from an organic matter into the air around it.

Easily measured, it came from the molecular charges between the organic matter and the air. Carbon releasing in decomposing tissue interacts with the air around it creating an increase in temperature. This is also the basic theory behind Global Warming.

Dr. Ma had not expected a reaction from any of the bodies to the poisoned bit of flesh. This was good news and bad news. The good news was that the human or Otherworldly being influenced by Circe to try and kill the tiger in South Africa was not one of the bodies in front of her.

This was also the bad news. It may mean a trip to South Africa in the near future to find that missing puzzle piece. If the piece was with the Sorceress, here and now, that would save Dr. Ma, David and Allistair, significant trouble finding it later.

Next, Dr. Ma took out the dried, blood soaked piece of fabric from the deck of Joseph's boat. Again, she didn't expect any reaction from the three bodies in a semi circle around her.

Unlike the three corpses in repose on their stainless steel sliding trays, she was sure the match to this scrap of tissue was long gone.

The evidence she had seen, led her to believe the first man from Miami was actually a snack for the Cetus that Circe brought with her. He had done his job and then provided an ancient sea creature with lunch. The trail she had seen that went into the ocean and straight down to the depths was her evidence of his demise.

He left in the belly of a beast, never to be seen again.

She had told Jeremy this much, minus the sea creature and the snack thing. Ma sighed and pulled out the last item she brought with her to the morgue. She look around at the puke green painted walls.

Stainless steel tables, refrigeration units, and their electrical hum competed with the flicker of the fluorescent light banks overhead.

Didn't they know that the fluorescent sources flickered up to 120 times per minute based on the power line voltage fluctuation in alternating current?

Migraines, seizures and plain old headaches were the results of this flickering for a small amount of the population. Imagine having to work in this depressing setting, death all around and a crappy paint job.

Then you get to add a daily headache, or worse, because of the lighting.

"Incandescent," she thought. Basic old hot glowing wire that didn't flicker due to AC changes.

Ma looked at the sphere and took a deep breath. "Get this over with," she thought. "Time to get out of here." She could hear Jeremy talking on his phone in the hallway. She hadn't taken much time up to this point.

Releasing the trapped Spirit Wind wouldn't take up much more. The worst effect would be on her.

She crushed the sphere in her hand and was immediately enveloped by the Spirit's departing message.

There was no need to have David's backup this time. The sphere was a diluted version that would move through her quickly. She simply needed to confirm there were no loose ends for Jeremy's investigation.

Her final plan was to remove Circe from the earthly plane for good. For peace of mind.

Dr. Ma hated loose ends. After two millennia of existence in this Elemental and human shared form, she had learned to close things up neatly whenever you could.

Not worth having anything come back to bite you in the butt because you were too lazy to handle it right the first time.

The message was just trickling away into the Ether when she heard a step behind her. "What is that you are holding Dr. Ma?" Jeremy's voice asked.

He stepped closer to look at the fragments of Allistair's shed skin in her palm.

"Yes, what *is* that you are holding?" came the voice of the suspicious M.E.

"Apparently you need an exterminator," Dr. Ma said, thinking quickly. She turned and pressed the skin remnants into the assistant's hand, effectively waking him from his semi fugue state.

The young man blinked and looked down into his hand with surprise.

"Is that some sort of *snake skin*?" the M.E. said, her voice rising.

Ma kept a hold of the assistants hand as she spoke, modifying his memory to the story she was presenting. "Yes," she said. "Your assistant has sharp eyes. He noticed it while he was waiting for me."

The assistant cleared his throat. It seemed as if he hadn't spoken in some time. "Yes ma'am," he said to the M.E. He looked over into the corner of the room as if he was having a hard time believing what he was saying himself. "I found it over there."

The M.E. was on the phone, yelling at someone about pest control and loss of integrity in her evidentiary process as Jeremy and Dr. Ma left.

"Thank you, Jeremy," Ma said as he walked her to her car. "I don't think I will need to go to Joseph's boat now, if you don't mind."

"That is fine Dr. Ma," Detective Brenner said. "Anything new for me?" he said hopefully.

"I believe I know something important about Joseph McCarthy's disappearance," she replied. "You are going to find him very soon."

"Alive," Brenner emphasized.

"Yes, I believe so," Dr. Ma responded.

They said good bye and Dr. Ma drove back to the clinic to share her discoveries with David.

Chapter Eleven - To Kill A Tiger

David was running along North County Road, breathing easy and moving fast, his usual 5 minute per mile pace.

Dr. Ma was not happy that he was still staying in his own apartment on the Island instead of with her at her more fortified residence, but he needed the space. Staying with her was a challenge for him.

Jeremy was still dating Karen. He saw them at Renato's last night. He knew Jeremy was the better choice for her. Not him. Never him.

He was a possible mate for Ma in the balance of Universal energy. But, they accomplished the balance just working together. They didn't have to be mates like she was with her first tiger balance.

Dragons mated for life and Ma was a dragon. Her first mate, a tiger, was not made the same as her though.

Tigers could be, and were, more fluid with mates. For example, when their original mate passed from this plane of existence. Unfortunately Ma didn't see things that way at all. David had all but given up hope that she ever would. He was noticing a bit more affection from her lately.

Perhaps she was just overprotective from his recent brushes with death. In his human form, not Elemental death. That type of demise was much harder to bring about.

He had wanted to make time to talk to her about what was going on, but now was not the right time. She was a bit distracted trying to kill a certain Sorceress.

Dr. Ma was obsessively searching for Circe. She knew that the Sorceress was still here, waiting to make her move.

Ma was sure she had tried to kill him in South Africa to throw the balance of power off and keep them from defeating her. Again. When they took her out a few hundred years ago in France, they hadn't expected her back so soon.

It had been David that took the lead in her downfall.

Each of them took out different bad guys and girls. As an Earth Element, David would be the lead in Circe's demise. His earthbound power would be her insurmountable challenge. She was an earth magic practitioner. So, she had tried to poison him. Ma took care of that.

Painful little treatment it was too. But, he had healed nicely.

He was flying along, his powerful strides propelling him forward to make the turn west where the road briefly jogged around the Breakers property.

He had passed several couples along his route. Holding hands, kissing in the sunny beachside atmosphere, happy. Quite a few looks came his way as he passed. Young women, older women, younger and older men.

Gold streaked blond hair flying lose over his shoulders and an incredible physical specimen gracefully negotiating the cars, people and pavement irregularities is what they were staring at.

Even among the usual flow of Palm Beach Island beauties, he stood out.

What did it matter really? He couldn't figure out human emotion, even after a millennia at his job protecting them. Their job, his and Ma's, not just his. Protecting humans from Otherworldly killers that was. Dr. Ma had been at it at least twice as long. She worked first with her original mate, another Elemental tiger.

He had a later start today at the clinic. Jet Carlson was taking over his Tai Chi class at the Mugen Dojo so he could come to Palm Beach and facilitate a women's self defense class at the Breakers.

He didn't know he would be creating a monster when he agreed to the Society of the Four Arts ladies club request to present a class for them. Dr. Ma was handling the patient load.

Winnie was about to strangle him for being absent so often from the clinic.

A Palm Beach Police officer had been handling the women's self defense class for a few years before his retirement. Detective Jeremy Brenner somehow got David roped into volunteering to do the class.

The proceeds went to the Police Department. David somehow got the class at the Breakers in the Summer *and* a class in the season for the Four Arts ladies.

He felt her presence almost immediately after he passed Royal Poinciana Way. He was heading north towards the quieter, more residential part of the famous island, but he was still in a stretch of shops and denser human activity.

Her unmistakable energy signature was strong and closing behind him.

"Ma, a little help!" he shouted in his head, knowing she would hear.

He picked up his pace as much as he dared without attracting too much attention from the humans around him. Circe was stalking him.

"Was she in the air?" he thought. "Far enough above him that humans wouldn't notice, yet close enough for him to sense her was possible." He felt her intent rather strongly.

It was not as if he couldn't fight her and win. He could. That was why she was so focused on trying to kill him first.

The problem was, that he and Ma were here to protect the humans all around him now. The runners, cyclists, dog walkers and steady line of drivers of cars, trucks and so forth. If Circe intended to launch an attack on him here and now, there would be human casualties.

David had a well honed warrior's mind. Battle strategy was almost instinctive. If the Sorceress was challenging him in a public setting, he would shift her focus to a less populated venue and take her on.

He quickened his pace as North County Road bore east and north again, leaving the last commercial areas behind. "I am moving too fast," he was thinking. Anyone watching would remember his speed as he passed.

He wanted less attention, not more. Close to 4 minutes per mile, he gritted his teeth and kept his desire to run faster in check.

"Ma?" he called again in his head. Not hearing her answer was a concern. The dragon was sure Circe had some new tricks up her sleeve.

Maybe one of them was blocking or delaying messages between Otherworldly beings. They could all hear each other. To a point. He and Ma were deeply linked. Their thoughts were more like an umbilical cord.

It was harder to *not* listen in than to hear each other.

"David!" he heard her answer him. It sounded far away, but he knew she would be coming to him from wherever she was.

He needed some help to give his battle with the Sorceress a cushion of protection from the human lives around him. Collateral damage was not acceptable.

The Sorceress would know he acted on that directive from his creator. She was using this to her advantage right now.

He took a westbound street, ending up flying westbound down Country Club Road after a few twists and turns.

He reached the 300 block of Country Club Road where it became North Lake Way and passed through the massive cut out rock formation that opened to the Intracoastal Waterway.

This was where North Lake Trail and North Lake Way ran side by side, northbound, along the west side of the Island. "Perfect," he thought. She was closer, he could almost smell her.

David reached the Intracoastal Waterway, and ran right into it. "Screw you bitch," he thought as he dove in. "I can fight in the water as well as on land. Bring it!"

If you had a glass observation window that showed David passing into the waterway above and below the surface, you would have seen a flawless transformation.

As his powerful human body broke the surface, the tiger appeared below it. In moments the massive beast was submerged in all his clawed, toothed and striped glory.

He heard their warnings too late. The Sorceress had been tamping down his reception of Otherworldly voices as he ran from her. The Water Sprites had been calling to him to stop. He hadn't heard them.

Nor could they get close enough for him to see them because of what waited between the rock shoreline and the deeper water.

He had turned back towards the shoreline to meet her onslaught when he felt it. A stabbing pain passing through him from his back to his front where the head of the spear appeared. David looked down in disbelief and turned around towards the waterway.

The Cetus. She had tricked him into believing she was the attacker, driving him into her trap. He felt the shock of magical energy from the weapon electrify his nervous system and arched backwards in pain.

No sound came from him. He couldn't move. He was dropping deeper into the water. He was going to drown if he couldn't get to the surface. His massive body was ignoring his commands.

Another jolt of energy made him gasp with pain, swallowing water and starting to choke.

He could hear the Water Sprites clearly now. Screams of fury came to him. It seemed the little creatures had launched an attack on the Cetus.

He saw it receding from his vision, a blur of activity around it. Few knew how fierce the little water dwellers could be when provoked. He felt another jolt and swallowed more water.

"I'm sorry An Ma," was the last thing he thought. An or peace, was his name for her since the beginning. He should have taken her warnings more seriously. Circe had grown strong and capable. At least enough to take out her enemy without laying a finger on him.

David felt something hit his back. He was laying on his side on the rocky coastline next to the Lake Trail. Dr. Ma was slapping his back hard enough to rupture a disc if he was truly human.

He didn't remember her pulling him out of the water. Coughing and then vomiting up dirty Intracoastal water made him look down at his now human body.

"When did I transform," he thought as another round of dirty water was evicted from inside of him. This time he noticed the arrowhead attached to the shaft sticking out of his abdomen.

God that hurt.

It didn't look like the spear the Cetus had skewered him with. It looked like a spearfishing bolt.

"Ma's work." He heard the sound of sirens pulling up on Country Club Road next to him. "She wouldn't have had time to hide me, so she changed the weapon into something humans would understand," he thought.

The Palm Beach Fire Department had state of the art equipment, including a Medical Rescue Unit staffed with highly trained personnel. They also didn't get a lot of awesome trauma calls. Like this one.

The medics surrounded him, pushing Dr. Ma back with their equipment boxes and stretcher. A bright yellow backboard made an appearance in front of him.

"We are going to get you to the hospital," the first medic said, establishing face to face patient rapport.

David wasn't really in much pain anymore. Once Dr. Ma changed the magical spear to a regular spearfishing bolt, his body started healing.

Besides, he could tolerate far worse than a spearfishing bolt through his body.

David nodded at the medic. He was sure to grimace in pain as they gingerly shifted him to the backboard and secured him and the bolt in place. No reason for them to think he was not reacting normally to his injury. Ma locked eyes with him as they loaded him onto the Medical Unit.

He winced again. The murderous fury in her head was deafening. She was going to rip Circe and her little sea pet to tiny shreds before setting them on fire was what he saw.

He had no doubt something was not going to go well for the Sorceress.

"I will see you at the hospital," she said silently in his head. "Try not to heal too quickly, let them remove the thing before your body manages to push it out."

"Got it," he answered just as silently. His view of her was suddenly obscured by a ginger haired, red faced, and almost as furious as Dr. Ma, Jeremy.

"Are you f-cking kidding me?" Brenner was sputtering as he looked at the bolt sticking out of David's abdomen.

"You are going to be fine, I swear to god I will find this idiot, are you guys en-route yet?" he said, all of it coming out in a rush.

"Jeremy," David said, teasing, but trying to calm his friend. "I didn't know you cared so much?" It came out a little weaker than his usual tone of voice.

After all, he did still have a fiberglass shaft stuck through his abdomen. Left on their own, Dr. Ma would have just snapped the end and torn the shaft out. He would bleed, but he would also heal rapidly.

Brenner's red face might have gotten a bit redder. A female medic asked him if he "intended to ride with them to the hospital or would he like to step out of their rig and let them go?"

Jeremy stepped out and joined Dr. Ma. The back door shut them out of David's view and he closed his eyes for the ride. He needed to focus on *not* healing. Great.

"Are you in pain?" the pretty female medic said, bending close to his face with a penlight. She was checking his pupillary response, cognition and from the smile she had, probably something more.

He was already hooked up to several things in the rig. Cardiac function, oxygen saturation and whatever else they could think of. Beeps and other noises said the machines were working.

David sighed and said, " I'm fine, really, no pain medication please." He noticed her prepping something for his IV. "I'm not a big fan of drugs."

Understatement of the year, really. Drugs may show the medics something they would never want to see. Delusional tigers were a big safety risk.

"You are doing great," she said, still smiling. "You look like, I mean according to your stats, you seem to be in great shape. If you are not in pain we won't push anything."

"Thank you," David said, closing his eyes and going back to his meditative focus to heal slower.

The pretty medic looked over her patient for more injuries. He was wet from the Intracoastal Waterway and sporting a spearfishing shaft from his abdomen but other than that he was incredible.

Powerful lean muscle under tanned skin and killer tattoos that wrapped his pelvis and lower back, diving down his buttocks under the snug running shorts. His eyes had been an unreal shade of lapis when he opened them to talk to her, his hair blond streaked, about shoulder length.

Dirty water from the waterway dripped a bit from his thick locks onto their rig floor. She dropped an absorbent pad with a plastic backing down under it. No need in one of them slipping.

He was stunning. She checked her clipboard. "What is your name?" she asked.

"David," he answered. Realizing she probably wanted more, he added "Anderson," and then rattled off his date of birth, address and phone number. Blood type, married or single and a few other questions followed. "She was making sure he wasn't losing consciousness or cognition," he thought.

Arriving at the hospital, they wheeled him past the entrance and the bank of intake rooms into an elevator.

"Where are we going?" he asked the pretty medic as hospital personnel joined them and started asking questions.

"Directly to radiology to see what we have and then probably into surgery to remove the bolt if everything looks fine," an new female voice answered.

A tall woman with blond hair pulled back in a severe bun and surgical scrubs was looking at the medic's chart. She had moved to stand directly in front of him. "Are you in pain?"

"Not too bad," he answered. This was moving a bit quicker than he expected. "I don't tolerate pain meds or general anesthesia, Dr.?"

"Jane Darden," she answered efficiently. "I am the trauma surgeon," she said frowning. "Depending on what is seen, we made need more tests, but soon you are off to surgery. Don't worry."

She turned to a nurse and handed her the chart. The elevator stopped and Dr. Darden stepped out with David and the nurse. The medics stayed behind for the trip back down.

"Doctor," David said making her look at him directly. He hated to do this, but he needed to make sure they didn't put him under.

"You don't want to put me under anesthesia," he said carefully and deliberately.

She held his gaze, almost without blinking. This was a predator thing, intimidating the prey. He didn't have Dr. Ma or Allistair's skills in thought manipulation, but he could do this.

"No," she said in agreement, eyes still locked with his. "We will only do what is necessary."

David blinked and looked away, effectively releasing her. Dr. Darden looked surprised for a moment as if she wasn't sure what happened.

The orderly that had met them at the elevator said, "Are you joining us in there?"

She indicated the room where an Interventional Radiologist name Yen was patiently waiting for the possible trauma.

"No," Darden said. She walked away, and called back over her shoulder, "call me if you need me, I think Yen can handle this." David sighed in relief.

Back at the scene, Detective Brenner was still sputtering in rage. The Chief of Police had arrived to comfort Dr. Ma. She was a well known philanthropist in their Town and David just as well known.

He was not happy that a resident and two important donors to Town charities were involved in a near fatal incident.

Dr. Ma had told Jeremy everything before the Chief arrived. Everything she was likely to tell him.

Brenner knew she was holding out on him, but they would talk later. Right now, in the presence of his departmental personnel, he was all business.

Detective Brenner briefed the Chief. "They were running north on Lake Trail Chief," he said. "The victim, Dr. David Anderson III, a Town resident, entered the waterway about here," he indicated the area where North Lake Trail began to run parallel to the Lake Trail walking path.

"He was going to swim a short section and rejoin Dr. Ma on the trail before they continued north towards the Sailfish Club."

The Chief took Dr. Ma's hand in his own and patted it lightly. "This must have been very traumatic for you to witness," he said. Chief Blont was a once, very good looking man, now aging well.

He had always considered himself a ladies man, even now. Dr. Ma had to give him credit for his skills in expressing concern and sympathy to her.

"No wonder he started in Road Patrol and moved so quickly." She smiled at him, encouragingly she thought.

"Yes, of course it was," he answered for her. "Detective Brenner is a top notch investigator, he will find the maniac who did this. There is absolutely NO spearfishing this close to our coast."

Jeremy broke in at this point, amazed that Dr. Ma was going along with the Chief's spiel so well. "The marine unit is in the water right now and we have a diver checking the area. Local agencies have been alerted. Dr. Ma said she didn't even see a dive flag."

Chief Blont dropped her hand to move off authoritatively. "Check every vessel in the area for evidence someone came onboard recently," he barked. "Walk the 'Trail' for any sign of someone coming out of the water and entering a residence or car on a side street."

The large grouping of officers around him moved off, doing his bidding. The same direction that had come from Detective Brenner only minutes ago.

"I'm sorry about the Chief and all of this Dr. Ma," Jeremy Brenner said softly to her. "I can have someone drive you to the hospital now if you like."

"No need, Jeremy," she said, pointing to the gleaming black BMW 7 series that had pulled up to the police blockade on Country Club Road and North Lake Trail.

Allistair McGowan got out of the back of it in a flawless three piece suit and tie. Brenner shouted to the officer who stepped forward to stop him.

"Mike! Let him through," he called to the young man in uniform. The cop changed his palm forward hand gesture to a wave through, even though Allistair hadn't yet slowed his pace.

Dr. Ma walked forward to meet her old friend and solicitor. "I can go now," she said carefully choosing her words in hearing distance of so many humans. "He seemed to be doing fine when they transported him."

Allistair got her meaning and replied, "Good enough, we will go right now." He stuck out a meaty hand to Detective Brenner. "Good to see you again Jeremy."

Brenner smiled. He liked the stuffy attorney. "You too Mr. McGowan. Look," he said. "I will take care of things here. Let me know when you are home Dr. Ma and I will come by and catch you up on the investigation."

"Thank you, Jeremy," Dr. Ma said and walked away to Allistair's car. His driver jumped out and opened the back door for her.

Detective Brenner grabbed Allistair's arm lightly as he followed her. "A word?" he asked the attorney. Allistair frowned slightly, partly at Jeremy's familiar touch and partly at the request.

"Yes?" he said a bit gruffly.

Brenner was not intimidated by anyone, so he just pushed on with what he had to say. "Dr. Ma was beside herself earlier. She calmed down after they took David away, but I think she would rip the shooter to shreds in front of all of us if she got the chance."

"Oh, good observation," Allistair said smiling. "That is *exactly* what she would do."

"Right," Brenner said. "When we catch this idiot, I just want to make sure someone keeps her from doing anything foolish. She is capable of doing a lot of harm and I don't want her to go to jail for killing someone."

"Ah," Allistair said, as if he was in on the conspiratorial tone of Brenner's revelations. "Dr. Ma is anything but foolish. She is however, a destructive force of significant power," he spoke truthfully. "If you or your police officers catch this, idiot, as you call him or her, I promise I will make sure she doesn't kill them, herself."

"Thank you," Brenner said to him, meaning it. "She was fierce when I got here."

"I bet she was," the attorney said, picturing the possible scene in his mind.

"I've got it from here. Oh, and Jeremy," he said as he walked away. "Just because you know her, doesn't mean you are safe from her when she gets like that."

He offered Brenner a smile and wave as he trotted off to join Dr. Ma in his car.
Brenner didn't know what kind of response went with that statement.

His investigative instincts told him the attorney was telling him the absolute truth. The detective shivered suddenly in the hot sun.

Turning back to the scene investigation, he tried to put what Allistair said out of his mind.

Allistair could easily keep his promise of preventing Dr. Ma from killing the perpetrator. "Because there is no way in hell you are going to catch the spear thrower," Allistair thought to himself.

"Nice guy," Allistair said to Dr. Ma as he sat next to her in the back seat. Leaning forward, he tapped the plexiglass panel between them and the driver to indicate they should leave.

Looking at Dr. Ma, he said, "Now tell me what in the hell is going on."

Chapter Twelve - Resurrection

"Put a rush on it," Dr. Ma said to Allistair. "He is doing fine so far with his predator/prey thing, but I need to make sure they don't put him under anesthesia without one of us there."

"Really?" Allistair said. "That cheesy, stare you into immobility, predator thing? Does that work well if you aren't planning to actually kill and eat them?"

He leaned forward to tap on the screen again. The driver increased his speed.

Ma slapped his arm. "Seriously, we don't need a massive tiger showing up in the O.R. Not that I think that will happen. I am more worried that he is healing too fast."

They arrived at the hospital and Dr. Ma quickly established herself as next of kin. Legally, she was his mother.

Allistair arranged for her to adopt him every time the tiger re-manifested. Then the attorney quickly produced paperwork from a fake medical doctor, citing David's extreme intolerance to anesthesia and pain medication.

All the lines of communication were buzzing to ensure their information was sent back to the doctor caring for the wounded tiger.

Dr. Darden was the first to respond. She walked into the family member conference room to greet Dr. Ma.

"Hello Dr. Ma, I'm Dr. Darden, the trauma surgeon on call. I reviewed your son's chart when he came and we sent him to Radiology. Dr. Yen determined the bolt was very superficial and I removed it. He refused a local anesthetic and didn't seem to been pain. He is a very lucky man."

"Thank you, Dr. Darden," Ma said smiling. "It looked worse on scene."

"You were there?" Jane Darden said, surprised. "I'm sorry, what field are you in?"

"David and I are Traditional Chinese Medical Doctors," Ma answered. "I have a Sports Medicine Practice and he specializes in Internal Medicine."

"You certainly look too young to have a son who is thirty five," Dr. Darden complimented her. "Your son is in amazing physical shape. I spoke with Dr. Yen and it seems that his dense musculature may have somewhat repelled the tip and shaft of the bolt so it circumvented the abdomen and remained superficial.

There was some slight tissue tearing of the right latissimus and obliques, an entrance and exit wound and minimal trauma."

"I've seen that type of deflection in trauma cases, but rarely," came another voice from the room's door. "Dr. Yen," a small Asian man introduced himself, walking in to join them.

"Dr. Ma," Ma introduced herself. "This is my solicitor, Allistair McGowen," Ma introduced her longtime friend.

"Everything went very well," the small man said, looking at Dr. Darden with an exasperated expression. "The medics seem to have greatly over stated the complexity of this injury. I haven't seen them do that before."

"Your son?" he said inquiringly, looking at Dr. Ma.

"Yes, my son," Dr. Ma agreed.

"You certainly look too young to have a son who is thirty five years old," he complimented her.

Dr. Ma smiled, "The staff here is certainly complimentary." Allistair was trying hard not to roll his eyes.

"He is going to be ready to take home very soon. Honestly, I saw more tissue damage in the images I took than when we actually visualized the area on extraction."

The man seemed perplexed. "We didn't insert a drain. There was minimal vascular damage. I think he will heal fine, but followup with a general practitioner."

"Well done," Allistair spoke up. "Better that it was overblown I say than underestimated. Dr. Ma will make a generous donation to the hospital. I am sure your respective areas could use some new equipment?"

Both physician's nodded, surprised at the turn of the conversation.

"Let's go," Dr. Ma said. "Point us in the right direction?"

Dr. Yen took the lead and brought them to the small recovery area where David pretended to rest on the uncomfortable hospital gurney. "Thank you, Dr. Yen," Ma said in flawless Mandarin as the small man began to walk away.

Yen smiled and replied, "Your son speaks Mandarin like a native, I guess I should have assumed you did as well."

Ma and Allistair turned their full attention to David as Yen left. Cringing slightly from the double set of glaring eyes, he said, "I'm sorry An Ma, you were right to think Circe would try again."

Allistair rolled his eyes this time now that nobody was looking. "When is she ever wrong?

We both know you can take the Sorceress one on one, but she wasn't going to play fair. She was trying to chip away at our strategy to evict her again. You are her main threat here on this plane of existence."

"Look at the trouble she went to in South Africa to try and poison you," Ma said. David looked downcast.

"Your job of slowing your healing went well, don't you think?" Ma teased, trying to lighten the mood.

David grinned sheepishly. "I really tried. I have never gone in reverse recovering from a near mortal wound. It's harder than you think."

"You're not mortal," Allistair commented.

"We need to get home," Ma said to them. "I have a plan but I can't discuss it here. We have some background work to do to make it real enough to fool Circe.

By the way, Jeremy is going to bust a seam if he doesn't see you tonight, but I have to keep him away."

"So," Allistair said, "It is going down tonight?"

"Yes," Ma replied. "Circe will take the opportunity to strike when we are weak. David and I that is. You Allistair, will be a big surprise among others.

"I am *not* weak," David objected.

"Give me a hard time about protecting you again," Ma snapped at him, "And you will find yourself needing another ambulance ride."

David and Allistair looked at each other. Never mess with the dragon when she was pissed off.

They got David signed out of the hospital and took him out the back VIP patient entrance. Checks to hospital administrators can do wonders.

The entrance was underground. If the Sorceress was in the air watching as David thought, she wouldn't see him get in the car.

Between the three Elementals in the glossy black luxury car, enough energy was able to be expressed to hide the inhabitants inside from anyone trying to see in. Even Circe.

Actually, they might have been able to cloak their movements from their own creator. Not that they would have.

Part of the acceptance of the check to the hospital administrator was Allistair's strict requirement that nobody at the hospital reveal David's condition.

He was assured that patient confidentiality was a top concern.

"Right," Allistair said as he got in the car. "We are leaving a clear trail for Circe to know we have David. Those humans couldn't hide their great grandmother's middle name from anyone the Sorceress would send to question them, so let's avoid that. Best she thinks we have him and he is in serious trouble that the humans don't know about."

"Why else would we rush him out of the hospital?" Dr. Ma said grimly. "I want her to think I am taking him to try and heal him in our own way."

They made the short trip to Dr. Ma's residence and rushed through the house and into the Library as fast as Berenice could get them there.

The Library was on a different plane of existence. All Circe or her minions would know was that he was no longer on the earthly plane.

"Cry, Berenice," Dr. Ma ordered the guardian spirit. "David is dying, so go up to my garden and cry like your heart is breaking. You need to convince whomever is watching."

Berenice looked up, shocked. She had hurried them all down to the Library. Ma had been carrying David since they got out of the car in her driveway to make the impression stick that he was in bad shape.

"But," she said looking at David standing there, "You look fine."

"I am fine Berenice," David said soothingly. "Dr. Ma is trying to fool Circe."

Berenice looked unsure. "If you can't act the part Berenice," Ma said, "I will gladly stab him again and make it seem real."

"Hey!" David said. Maia stepped in front of him as if to hold off any attack.

"I can do it!" Berenice said and returned to Ma's garden. Her little stone statue in the Library became still. They could hear her wailing from there. It echoed in the mirror image of her fountain in front of them.

"Nice," Allistair observed. "Were you really going to stab him? I would pay money to see that."

"Hey!" David objected again.

"Enough," Ma said. "Here is my plan to bring down the Sorceress. She is going to disappear this time. For good."

Couches, chairs, a table with a glass and a decanter of brandy all appeared for them to use. "I know you are hungry David," Ma said, preempting David's complaint about no food appearing.

Maia walked in a few minutes later with a tray heaped with raw and steamed vegetables, nuts, seeds and sprouted rice.

"Thank you, An Ma," David said, heaping food on the plate before sitting down.

"I am surprised you made it out of the hospital without finding some ogling female to bring you something to eat," Ma teased.

"He does just as well with ogling men." Allistair added slyly.

"Personal observation, Allistair?" Ma laughed.

"Hey!" David said for the third time since they arrived in the Library. He was too busy eating to manage much more.

"Okay," Ma said, "this is how are going to get her."

A whiteboard and erasable marker appeared in the middle of their little gathering as she stood up. She picked up the marker and started to draw her battle plan on the three by five foot board.

David had finished eating. He sat back on the couch. Maia settled in next to him, picking up his legs and feet to stretch them over her lap, the length of the couch.

David looked distinctly uncomfortable but didn't have the heart to pull away. Besides, her rubbing his legs and feet felt great. Spirit form not withstanding, she could exert real pressure on his tired body.

Allistair rolled his eyes at the display and poured another brandy.

"You pick on Brenner about his notepad and you are using a whiteboard and marker?" David teased Dr. Ma.

Dr.Ma ignored him as she outlined her plan. "Circe will be drawn to us here," she said, pointing to her diagram. She had drawn her residence location, South Flagler Drive, and an area around Jamil's tree. She also included the east third of the Intracoastal Waterway that bordered the area.

"I will go for a walk tonight alone and stop by Jamil's tree," Ma said, placing her first X. She always used an increasing number of X's to indicate phases of a battle strategy.

"Allistair, you will slip into the Intracoastal from my backyard and make your way to the area just east of Jamil's tree. The Cetus will be in place ahead of her arrival, I am sure of it, so don't arrive too early.

Allistair nodded his assent, sipping his second brandy. He was feeling a bit hungry, but he couldn't have a large meal now. He would have to wait. Being hungry made him a bit edgy. Too bad for the Cetus.

He vaguely wondered what Cetus tasted like. "Can't be great." he thought. "Ancient and like seaweed probably."

"I will be here," Ma said, marking a spot next to Jamil's tree. "I will have the Guardian obscure the area while we engage the Sorceress so there will, hopefully, be no human collateral damage."

"Waterway?" David said, more in clarification than interruption. He was sure she would have it covered, he just wanted to know how.

"Tam will be north and south of the area in tandem with the Water Sprites creating an arc of obfuscation."

"Obfuscation?" Allistair said. "I thought that only applied to spoken word."

"They will be speaking the words, Allistair," Ma said. "You don't remember how to harness wind?"

Before either of them could delve deeper, David said, "Stop! Who cares what it is called as long as it works?"

Maia seconded his comment, smiling at him as she dug her fingers into his shoulders, rubbing out the muscle knots. David had to stop a groan of pleasure from escaping his lips.

Allistair grinned at him. "Were you going to leave these two alone here for even a short period of time?"

David blushed and Maia stopped her ministrations. Dr. Ma just laughed. "They will come through. I can always arrange for him to come back later."

Maia smiled and David looked even more embarrassed. Ma continued outlining her plan. "David will be here with Maia and Berenice," she said. Maia frowned slightly at this revelation. Ma continued, "I will call Avo," she said.

At this, David, Allistair, Maia and even Berenice turned to stare at her incredulously. "What?" was the collective question from all four of them.

Ma looked at all of them slowly and deliberately. "Avo has made a few non manifestation appearances here on this plane. I didn't know about it until I looked into the book of Otherworldly appearances. I was trying to track who and what Circe may be working with.

But, he cannot manifest here unless David were dead."

Ma and David looked at each other intently, each trying to hear the other's thoughts on the subject.

Dr. Ma, as usual, won. "I don't want you dead David or I would have let Circe kill you."
"That is comforting," David said.

Dr. Ma sighed. "I can call him to me on the earthly plane if you are here in the Library. There will be no shift in the Universal balance unless you are both on the earthly plane."

"My job would be?" Allistair said, clearing his throat. He was feeling left out of the actual battle at this point.

"Kill the Cetus," Dr. Ma said simply. " I will keep it distracted if I can, and you will finish it off."

"Literally finished off?" Allistair said, looking uncomfortable. "You are always asking me to eat some unpalatable thing these days. I am hungry though."

"Yes, probably," Ma said. "I don't want to leave ocean sea monster remains in the Intracoastal Waterway and you are the only Elemental close enough to ask to dispose of him.

"Yuck!" David commiserated. Allistair nodded glumly. "What about me?" David said. "Where do I fit into your plan?"

"I don't know," Dr. Ma said thoughtfully. "I will call for you when and if I need you. Maia is capable of transporting you to and from the library at least once without my help. I may not need you at all if Avo comes when I call him. I need his power to transport Circe to her new home."

David took this last bit of Ma's plan poorly. His heart dropped, a strange feeling taking over his chest and limiting his breathing.

He wasn't exactly sure, but he thought it may be jealousy tinged with the feeling he was being replaced with Dr. Ma's lost mate.

If she didn't call him and Avo stayed on in the earthly plane, what would he do? He couldn't return to his old life. That would belong to Avo.

He couldn't wait here in the Library forever could he? Not without dying of boredom and loneliness. A great massage and whatever Maia intended to come with it would not be enough.

He would rather die in the battle and let Avo regain his place with Ma.

"Maia," Ma said suddenly. "May I speak with you a moment?" The two got up and passed though a door that appeared in the wall of the room they were sitting in. Simply appeared as they walked towards it.

The Library held so many secrets.

"She is really playing for some tiger," Allistair said to David after Dr. Ma and Maia left.

"Who?" David asked. "Maia?"

"A bit slow on the uptake, right? Cats aren't terribly smart I understand?" Allistair teased. "We are leaving you two here for what may seem like hours on the earthly plane. How about including Berenice?" he said, lowering his voice. "Can you handle the two of them?"

"I can hear you, snake," Berenice said from her fountain. "Maia and I are not interested in the tiger."

"Please," Allistair snorted.

Dr. Ma and Maia reappeared. "All set, let's go Allistair."

David got up from the couch and came to stand by Dr. Ma. He looked at her carefully, thinking he may never see her again if Avo decided to stay on in his place.

The older Elemental tiger was more powerful. David wouldn't win in a contest of who stayed with Ma.

"Oh, David," Ma said. "One last thing before I go. You aren't completely healed and I will need you one hundred percent if I call you."

David looked at her, waiting for her to explain what she was going to do.

From behind him, he felt Maia move, and before he could get away, she draped a long tube of Allistair's previously shed snake skin over his head. She quickly pulled it down over his body.

Maia had a large store of it to make covers for some of the Library's more delicate tomes.

The spelled skin molded itself over him, binding his arms and legs.

Ma stepped up to him and kissed him lightly on the forehead before he could object. He slipped to the floor and into unconsciousness.

"Was that necessary?" Allistair said, frowning.

"Yes," Dr. Ma said. "He would never have stayed here voluntarily. I needed to know he wouldn't move a muscle until I was ready for him. Besides, he really will heal completely in there, you know that."

"I suppose you are right," Allistair sighed, looking at David cocooned in his shed skin, lying on the floor between them. "But, he is going to be pretty pissed off at you when he wakes up."

"Always possible," Ma replied. She looked at Maia with her most intense glare. Even Allistair winced. "Don't you dare be a moment late," she said to the nervous looking entity. Maia just nodded, mute.

Grabbing Allistair's hand, Ma dipped her fingers in Berenice's fountain and they arrived in her garden. It was almost time.

They just had a few more things to take care of.

Chapter Thirteen - Circe and the Cetus

It was time to put her plan into action. Dr. Ma stood beside Jamil, her ancient friend. "I need your help Jamil," she said to the face, barely recognizable in the brown and grey crumpled skin.

A moment passed. What appeared to be the time worn remnants of tree limbs, long ago broken away, opened, revealing lapis blue eyes. Jamie blinked slowly.

"Is it time?" he said in his slow, sonorous voice. Jamil and the tree were not one.

The ancient guardian used the tree as his residence to watch over a key ley line running through Florida, and, to help Dr. Ma when needed it seemed. "I feel her coming," he said.

"Yes," Ma answered grimly. "She will be here very soon."

Jamil's ancient Florida Sand Pine seemed to shiver, its branches swaying slightly with an unfelt breeze. Jamil was rousing himself to help her fight.

"I am ready," Jamil said louder now. His voice seemed to be coming from the air all around the tree.

She knew his essence was no longer fully bound within the tree's confines. His powerful magic would be in use. Jamil was supposed to be neutral.

He could not directly help her in the coming battle with Circe. He could however, be a Guardian. The atmospheric pressure changed around her, Jamil was changing the battlefield so humans would not become involved in what was about to happen.

If a human was driving their car, riding their bike, or walking their dog, they would inexplicably change direction away from that particular area of Flagler Drive.

If one of the human inhabitants of the houses facing where they stood, thought to look out their windows or sit on their front porches, they would find themselves in a mild fugue state, unable to focus on their surroundings.

There would be a strong urge to go back inside and do something else.

Soft splashes sounded behind her, along with a susurrus of wind, that didn't reach where she was standing.

She looked out on the Intracoastal Waterway to see a group of Water Sprites, arranged in a large arc from the concrete abutment wall by Jamil, out into the waterway and back.

At the apex of the arc was a small wave, in motion, yet not moving. On it stood Tam, smiling.

Ma knew they would provide the same function that Jamil was. No direct interference in the battle to come, just a protection from human involvement.

Anyone negotiating the waterway while the fight was ongoing, would detour around the area defined by the Sprite arc and Tam. They would surely think nothing of it and never remember doing so after they had passed.

Ma nodded her head, "Thank you all," she said. "Lets begin, we are almost out of time."

Ma stood on the concrete abutment wall between Jamil and the waterway, arms spread wide, palms facing the tepid skyline. "Avo!," she intoned deeply, "I call you!"

A moment passed, in which the air around her shimmered and crackled with energy. The sky seemed to brighten. All around her complete silence reigned.

He was coming.

The shimmer of the air became a vibration. She felt an increasing pressure in her ears. Then, the fabric of the earthly plane in front of her split with a resounding thunderclap.

Not a single Otherworldly being on the planet could have missed that sound. Ma smiled grimly. "Screw you Circe," she thought. It was too late for the Sorceress to change her mind now.

Suddenly, he was standing there. Just a few feet from her on the wall, in all his terrible beauty and power. Her mate, lost so long ago.

He was supposed to never return to her in this plane and upset the balance. Not unless David died, and left her forever. She had no choice but to call him to her now.

The Sorceress must be defeated, again. She had grown strong.

"Ama," he called to her softly. She stared at him, fixing his face in her memory again, like it was now.

Behind her an explosion out of the Intracoastal Waterway revealed the Cetus rising out of the water, snapping its jaws in their direction.

"That must mean," Ma thought almost in tandem with Avo, as they both looked the opposite direction from the Cetus, "she is coming from this direction."

She was. Circe appeared, arms outstretched and draped in human skins that wrapped around her loosely.

"Disgusting creature," Ma thought as she noticed the Sorceress' attire. She met Avo's eyes momentarily, as easily as if they had just fought side by side yesterday. A thousand years apart slipped away. They both grinned. "Bring it on," Ma said, and jumped backwards to engage the Cetus.

Avo mirrored her words silently as he leapt towards Circe, transforming seamlessly into the massive tiger of her memories.

Like David, Avo was steel grey with black stripes. His brilliant lapis blue eyes glowed from the yellow ring surrounding the iris. Ma heard a sound she hadn't heard for a millennia.

A powerful scream ripped from the tiger's throat. His primal scream. His battle cry.

The Earth Element tiger, choosing the earthbound Sorceress, and the Air Element Dragon, choosing the water bound Cetus to fight. Balance in battle.

Not at all what Circe had planned.

The Cetus snapped its powerful jaws all around the dragon. Ma had transformed as she leapt into the air, her powerful wingspan lifting her easily out of its reach.

She would let the creature tire itself out before going in for the kill. Ma darted just close enough to the creature's powerful jaws and front talons to make it lunge at her, then, she quickly retreated.

"Fly, you overgrown fish," Ma taunted it.

Cetus were very similar to dragons with front legs and wings, but, their lower body was more of a serpent, one long tail ending in a split, webbed fork like a scorpion.

She knew their leathery smallish wings were for speed in the water, not air flight. She was biding her time, waiting for Allistair to arrive and enact her plan.

Avo, meanwhile was nearly besting the Sorceress with a flurry of massive, sharp teeth and claws. His physical strength was a match for her magic.

Ma was just waiting for Allistairs' arrival to tip the balance of power.

Avo and Circe were battling fiercely on Flagler Drive, right in front of Jamil's tree. Magical sparks were flying from her, saliva and blood from him as he tore through her defenses again and again.

She had done him some physical harm, but, in his Elemental state, she would have to do a lot better to kill him.

He healed even as he fought. Ma watched as Circe drove a magical spear through Avo's back flank. He screamed in fury and pain. Ma's first instinct was to kill Circe's ocean beast below her and go to him.

A huge, green, Anaconda now rose from the water directly behind the Cetus. Ma distracted the Cetus, moving it in her direction. It hadn't seen Allistair yet.

Massive coils of green began wrapping around the sea monster's body. The Cetus turned its ugly head towards the green serpent behind it and lunged.

Ma exhaled a blast of fire, engulfing its upper body. The Cetus screamed, writhing and trying to submerge itself in the water. Alistair held it aloft, allowing it to burn.

"Ouch," came Allistairs' comment in her head. "This is not a cookout, I like my meat raw."

"Sorry," she sent back. She watched the Great Python wrap a final coil around the serpent before pulling it underwater. It wouldn't drown, but Allistair obviously didn't want to swallow a flaming shish kebob.

Turning her attention back to Avo and Circe, she heard a subtle tear in the fabric behind their battle scene.

"Finally," Ma though with relief. As David stepped through, Ma rushed forward. "Maia!" she cried out silently to the librarian. She was holding the Universal fabric open for David to step through. "Hold the door!"

David, immediately reached for Circe in front of him as she aimed another magical spear at Avo.

David's transformation was only partial as his claws tore into her back and pulled her towards the opening. It was enough. The Sorceress was completely taken by surprise.

Avo turned towards Ma as he heard her call to the librarian. His eyes grew wide as he saw her rushing towards him. Her intent was clear.

He had seen David step through the door, felt the crazy tilt of the Universal balance as the both of them were briefly present on the earthly plane.

"Why?" was all he got out as he and Circe were both tossed through the opening to another plane of existence. Maia had been in on the plan from the beginning. Her son Hermes' skills of travel were inherited from his mother.

She not only handled the delivery of David with ease but would ensure a smooth and fast eviction of Circe and Avo from the earthly plane.

Ma had requested a split travel plan, so as not to leave Avo battling with Circe alone in some alternate plane.

Where they each were going, Ma didn't care to know. As long as they were gone. She felt guilty for using her former mate without his permission to trap the Sorceress.

She was sure he thought she was calling him back to her. Of course, David would have had to have died.

She didn't know why Avo being happy about that circumstance caused her so much anger towards him.

She looked at David and dropped her Elemental form to embrace him. His tiger elements faded rapidly. "Welcome back," she greeted him.

He held her tightly, not wanting to let her go. The battle, the danger, their nearness, it was overwhelming. He bent his face closer to hers.

"Ahem," came from just behind them. Allistair stood there in one of his meticulously tailored suits, brushing water droplets off his lapel.

"Get a room, will you?" he said dryly. "Jamil and the waterway crew would like the world around us to go back to normal now."

David quickly let Ma go, embarrassed at having almost kissed her in front of so many Otherworldly beings who were still working to assist them.

"What are you doing?" he thought to himself. He knew that he and she were not likely to ever be intimate.

For her part, Ma had stepped away from him quickly, all business now.

She thanked the others for their work and told them to let go of the control they exerted over the humans perceptions around them.

David looked up just as Tam gave him thumbs up. He flushed slightly, feeling it may have been about his poorly thought out moment with Dr. Ma. Tam had been deposited on the concrete abutment and was now riding off on one of his many high end bicycles.

The Sprites were disappearing in small barely audible pops into the waterway and Jamil gave him a long look before closing his tree eyes.

The three of them standing there made an interesting group. Ma was dressed in black training gear, Allistair in a suit meant for the office and David in the running shorts he had on after the hospital visit.

Being cocooned in snakeskin hadn't given him an opportunity to change before Maia delivered him to the battle from the Library's dimension.

They all looked relieved to say the least. Maybe a bit worse for wear. Ma reached over and wiped a dried smear of what looked like Cetus blood from Allistair's lapel.

"You should try to transform a little further away from a kill," she said smiling at him.

David was busy trying to appear nonchalant.

"Still embarrassed by that post battle greeting?" Ma said to him, teasingly. Allistair grinned broadly, causing David's cheeks to flush.

He didn't respond to either of them. He was still pretty pissed off that Ma had tricked him into staying out of the battle until the very end.

"Dinner?" Allistair suggested jovially. The three walked slowly to Dr. Ma's home, just down the street from where they stood.

Chapter Fourteen - Finding Joseph

"I am surprised you found me so easily," Joseph McCarthy said to Dr. Ma.

"I have my sources," Ma replied carefully.

They were sitting at a table by the glass french doors of the outdoor restaurant at Long Wharf. Joseph had chosen to temporarily hide out in his friend's yacht in Sag Harbor, New York.

The Waterfront Marina could accommodate large yachts and the one sitting there was one of the largest.

"Only the best," Ma though about Joseph's choice. A very distinctive 193 foot Dutch made yacht, the INTUITIVE boasted a 14 member crew, a helicopter landing pad and many other amenities.

It currently belonged to a close friend and associate of the Palm Beach billionaire , but Joseph could have easily leased it, were it available.

The restaurant they were sitting in wasn't even open for the season yet. They were the only diners. The chef from the yacht was in the back, preparing them a light lunch. Ma wasn't interested in dining on board.

The Air Elemental got slightly seasick on even a large vessel like the luxury yacht in front of her.

The air was still chilly, so both of them wore long pants and sweaters despite the tall propane heater crackling cheerfully a few feet away.

"So," Ma began, "How did you get involved in this mess?"

Joseph McCarthy shifted uncomfortably and paused before answering her. "I met a woman a few years back, and we had a hot and heavy thing for a few weeks," he said. "Are you sure she is dead? I don't want to have to look over my shoulder for her crazy a— when I get home."

"Killed in an accident in Turkey," Ma fibbed. "She was never in Palm Beach. My solicitor tracked her to make sure we had the right one. She may have just hired men to carry out her orders regarding you."

Joseph sighed, apparently relieved. Then he looked up. "I think she was going to have me killed if I didn't go with her."

"Back to when you met her," Ma prompted. "You were married at the time." She showed no sympathy for his 'almost' demise.

Cheating bastard. Poor Ann. Ma knew what it was like to be faithful to one love for a very long time.

"Yes," Joseph said. "Ann and I have been married for 50 years next week." He looked at her intently, his eyebrows almost touching as he frowned.

"We all cheat on our wives," he said, as if in explanation. "The point is, to never embarrass them. This crazy b-tch, Celina, was like some fatal attraction thing. She wanted me to leave Ann."

"This is great," Ma thought to herself. "Circe was after Joseph McCarthy for personal reasons! I can't wait to tell Allistair and David this one."

Her face betrayed no emotion on the outside, despite her inner enjoyment of the tale.

"Anyway, I broke it off and she told me I would regret it, blah blah blah, you know how women are," he said.

Looking up suddenly, he realized she was a woman. "I'm sorry, no offense," he half apologized.

"None taken," Ma said, truthfully, she wasn't really a human woman at all.

"I hadn't heard from her since then, until about a week before I left. She called and said she was coming to Palm Beach, and that she was going to leave with me, or bury me. Of course, I planned a quick exit before she could arrive."

"So Ann knew you were coming here?" Ma asked.

"Yes and no," he said. "On my boat yes, but I arranged to stay here way ahead. I was going to go to my boat and tell the Captain last minute to go without me and tell nobody.

I had a ride arranged with a guy from Miami, who hired some criminal type to take my place on the boat. To give the impression I was there without really being seen."

"What tipped you off that something was wrong?" Ma asked, getting more interested in the details of Joseph's saga.

"When I got there and dropped off the dupe, I was still sitting in my car and I thought I heard a gun shot. There was nobody around but my crew and Captain. I know gunshots, and this sounded like one. I got the willies and told my guy to drive off, fast. I never got out the car to check on the crew or Captain." Joseph paused, thinking.

"It looks like your Captain shot one crew member he had with him, shot a second one later and then killed the *dupe*, as you call him, even further away," Ma said, giving him the details he was missing.

"They found the body of the first crew man floating south of the Marina and the second crew man tangled up on the shoreline plants almost to the north end of Palm Beach Island. The dupe's body has not been found."

"What about the Captain?" Joseph asked. "I think he was working with Celina. She has some deep criminal connections. His voice sounded strange when I called to make sure he was ready to go."

"When your boat was found, partly moored in a small un-named islet chain halfway to the Bahamas," Ma explained, "he had been dead for a few days."

"She killed him," Joseph stated firmly. "She could have it done. You said there was evidence on the boat?"

"Detective Brenner is working the case in Palm Beach," Ma said. "I am sure he will fill you in when you get home. By the way," she added, "He is dating your daughter again."

Joseph looked up, his face clouding over. "I don't approve of her seeing some low prospect cop. I was hoping she and David would eventually hit it off. What happened there?"

"The South Africa trip hit a glitch and I think she was a bit traumatized," Ma said. "Good thing you sent David with her or I think you would be childless. David has certain, ah, skills."

Joseph's eyes widened. Ma wished she hadn't been so blunt. "She is fine of course. It may have involved this Celina woman. Their campsite was attacked by armed men. They also could have been local criminals, but they were well outfitted. My solicitor flew them out

284

privately and Karen didn't have a scratch on her. She did stop seeing David and start seeing Jeremy almost immediately. Trauma changes you."

"I know," Joseph said, looking away, out into the Marina. Their Cobb salads and poached fish in dill had come and gone.

Ma was sipping a sparkling water while Joseph was on his second scotch. "I had better get home and get things settled," he said finally.

"My corporate jet is on the runway waiting for us," Ma said.

"One of two planes," Joseph said, finishing his drink and standing up. He held out his hand to help her up, very old fashioned gentlemanly behavior she noticed.

"My assets aren't public," Ma said quietly.

"I have friends in low places," Joseph said by way of explanation.

"Yes, I am sure you do," Ma said, smiling slyly as they walked to her waiting car. The driver had been sitting there, keeping it running and warm while they were inside. "I meant what I said, my assets are not public."

Joseph McCarthy helped Dr. Ma into the back of the Town Car and walked around to get in beside her from the other side. "Yes," he thought, she *was* interesting. She means I have only uncovered the surface regarding her wealth.

All the more reason he preferred David for his daughter Karen.

Joseph knew that Dr. Ma was David's legal guardian after his parent's died. How, he didn't know, but David was wealthy in his own right. Ma's wealth may eventually benefit the stunningly handsome young man as well.

He would have to eliminate the cop as soon as he got home. Eliminate him from Karen's life that was, Joseph didn't deal in the other kind of elimination. Anymore, that is.

The car pulled out of the parking area slowly and headed for the East Hampton Airport. Back in Palm Beach, Detective Brenner was at the McCarthy residence, delivering the news to Ann and Karen that Joseph had been located in Sag Harbor.

He pulled the missing persons bulletin as soon as Dr. Ma called him this morning. He didn't even want to know how she managed to find him.

The official story so far was that Joseph left suddenly on a emergency business trip to the Hamptons by private jet. He was going to take his boat but time was pressing so he had the boat Captain follow him up the coast.

He sent a message to the boat to return without him when he realized he would be longer than expected.

Joseph never received an answer from the man because he was dead. No answer was not a cause for alarm. Joseph did not expect an answer necessarily, just for the man to do his job.

The Captain never returned, so couldn't relate to Ann McCarthy her husband's revised itinerary. Plausible if not actually true.

To keep the lie going, Brenner was told that Joseph didn't know about his missing person status until notified by a family friend today. He was well and en-route home to Palm Beach by private jet. End of report.

No followup needed. Just the murder and suspicious death related to Joseph's boat.

He had a great alibi in the private jet and yacht crew. There had been no mention that the driver that took him to the airport was anything other than a regular car for hire. No need to follow that up based on Joseph's timeline.

Besides, the man said the Captain had arranged for the car, and he was dead.

Detective Brenner related all this to Joseph's wife and daughter. Ann McCarthy looked like she had dropped 20 years by the time he finished.

"He will be landing at Palm Beach International Airport later today," was the last thing Brenner said.

Ann McCarthy nodded and then excused herself. As she left, she looked over her shoulder at Karen and Jeremy.

"Thank you, Detective Brenner," she said in her soft, New England cultivated accent. "Let me do something for you in return dear."

Brenner looked at her curiously. He caught Karen's face turning red out of the corner of his vision.

They were sitting on a few formal chairs at the base of the front hall's winding double staircase. Ann McCarthy was on the right side staircase, heading for her and her husband's wing of the richly appointed residence.

"My husband, Joseph, doesn't approve of Karen dating you," Ann said bluntly.

Jeremy marveled that it still sounded like something good had been told to him in her softly accented voice.

"You two may want to get in one last good time before he gets home." Ann paused and looked at her daughters wing of the house. You had to go left up the staircase from where they stood.

Ann walked away as Jeremy stood there speechless. "She is very direct," he managed to get out after a moment or two.

"My father wants the best for me," Karen tried to explain. "He just doesn't think you make enough money."

"He is right," Brenner agreed. "I always say we need a raise in salary." His attempt at lightheartedness was failing. "If you wanted money, why not stick with David?"

Karen looked away answering, "There is something wrong about David. I really can't explain it. Think about why he is alone, looking like that and that rich."

Brenner held in a sudden need to defend his friend. He did what he did best. He said nothing, waiting for her to continue.

She turned back to face him. "Let's just see how things go when he gets home," she said. "I will bring up seeing you when he is settled in."

Brenner suddenly remembered Dr. Ma's statement about not getting attached to Karen. "How does she even know these things?" he asked himself, not for the last time.

Hiding his disappointment, he gave Karen a neutral smile and said "Sure, call me when you know what you want."

He turned away from her and walked towards the front door. She caught up with him in a few steps. Grabbing his arm she pulled it around her and pressed her lips to his. "Please don't go," she whispered. "We have some time before he gets here."

Jeremy Brenner extracted himself gently from her embrace. "Honestly Karen," he said as he opened the heavy wooden front door. "Unless you"re interested in an actual relationship, I think I'll skip a quick hookup."

She just stood there, staring at him as he closed the door.

The weather was turning warmer again in South Florida. Jeremy pulled off his sport blazer and hung in on the hook in the back seat of his unmarked police car.

Getting in the driver's seat, he looked back to the closed front door. It suddenly dawned on him that he had sounded like a modern day Rhett Butler from Gone With the Wind.

"Well frankly Karen," he said to himself, "I really don't give a damn."

The practical Irish kid in him had had enough of their on again, off again relationship.

Jeremy was a simple man, confident in his life's choices, for the most part. "A nice girl will come along when she is ready," his mother had recently said to him.

"A nice girl who doesn't mind dating a poor cop," he added out loud. Ma had been right. Karen was just clinging to him as the only port in the storm when her father was missing.

He pulled out of the McCarthy's driveway and headed back to the police department.

Karen's comments about David were still bothering him. His friend and martial arts teacher was a good guy. He may be different, and that was an understatement, but he was kind and compassionate to everyone.

"Screw you Karen," he thought.

Parking along Australian Avenue, the amount of cop cars was too much to fit in the department's small underground and east lot slots, he got out and looked around at the beautiful day.

Time for a quick walk to Starbucks on Worth Avenue. He had been busting his butt on this complicated case. There was still plenty to be done before he could file everything away as completed. A caramel macchiato would do the trick.

A short time later, Dr. Ma's small private jet landed at Palm Beach International Airport's General Aviation and disembarked its passengers. Her gleaming red Mercedes sat, waiting for her, on the area just off the tarmac.

She and Joseph got in and she headed towards Palm Beach. The McCarthy residence was just off Worth Avenue, on the south end of South Lake Drive.

For the short 20 minute drive, Joseph McCarthy didn't say a word. He had been silent the entire plane ride back as well. Except to ask for a couple more scotches. Neat.

When Dr. Ma pulled into his driveway and stopped, he asked her to come in. She politely declined. "Its time to get your life settled with just your wife and daughter right now," she said.

He looked at her, clearly processing something in his head. Ma was too polite to listen in if it wasn't necessary. She could have though, but why bother?

"I don't know exactly what your involvement was in this whole thing," he said carefully, watching her reaction. "I do know I owe you. Big. I am a powerful and influential man, Dr. Ma.

"You seem very capable of taking care of your life, but someday you may need something from me. I won't forget what you have done for me. Just ask."

Ma stared back at him intently, her brilliant lapis blue eyes seeming not to blink. "I will collect from you someday, Joseph," she said. "I am sure of it. Do good things with what you have amassed in this life. It's the least you can do with your second chance."

He looked at her a minute more. Her blue eyes seemed to touch a primal fear deep in his soul, but he couldn't decide exactly why. He nodded and got out of her car, closing the door gently and walking up to his front door.

Ma watched the front door open and Karen fly out. "She must have been watching for him to arrive," Ma thought. She smiled as they embraced. Ann was standing quietly in the doorway.

Ma was sure their greeting would be less effusive, and in private.

Exiting their driveway north on South Lake Drive, Ma took the immediate right onto Peruvian. She pulled up in front of Renato's back entrance a few moments later. David was waiting for her on the sidewalk, smiling. She had texted him when the plane landed at PBIA.

"He is so incredibly handsome," she thought, taking in the elegantly attired younger man waiting for her.

Perfectly tailored tan slacks and a button down white cotton shirt set off his golden skin and wavy blond hair. The sun streaks were more noticeable when he wore his shoulder length hair loose as he did now. A navy Ralph Lauren sport blazer was casually draped over one arm.

He walked towards her car as she got out, holding the other arm out to her. This was just his old fashioned way of escorting her whenever they went out to an event or just dinner, as they were tonight.

"He smells delicious" she thought guiltily. "So male, warm and sexy." She paused looking up at him. "I made the right decision," she said, not realizing she was speaking aloud.

David looked startled for a moment. Then he realized she was talking about choosing him over her lost mate Avo in the battle with Circe. Ma could have easily kept Avo and turned the tables on him, pushing him through the Universal rip with the Sorceress.

He bent his 6'5" frame slightly, after all, Ma stood a good 6' herself and more in heels, and kissed her gently on the forehead. He resisted the urge to kiss her elsewhere. He wasn't sure that was the right move to make with her.

Maybe, just maybe, they would get there one day. They looked at each other for a moment longer before turning to head towards Renato's outdoor seating and a relaxing dinner.

Chapter Fifteen - The Library

"Okay, David," Ma said. "We are, all three of us, are going to spend some time in the Library."

David had wondered why Allistair had shown up early on the first Saturday of their week long vacation. Dr. Ma had asked him to stay over last night after dinner.

Nothing intimate had happened, but they had curled up on her couch together and watched the second installment of that witches and wizards movie series.

The two of them were more convinced than ever that the author was an Otherworldly. Hopefully they could find someone who knew her that could tell them exactly what *kind* of Otherworldly she was.

David also wondered what exactly Dr. Ma and he were going to do with their time for an entire week off. They were not exactly the hang out and relax kind of duo. They liked to have something to do.

Humans with a limited lifespan relaxed. Theirs was endless. Downtime was inevitable.

The Palm Beach Police Department had insisted their busiest detective take some of his vacation time. Jeremy Brenner had gone home to Ireland for a week, to visit family and reconnect with his roots.

David jokingly had commented that the roots better not include too much alcohol and crappy food, or he was going to make sure Jeremy suffered in martial arts class when he got back.

Jeremy had been a student at Dr. Ma and David's martial arts school, the Mugen Dojo, every since they helped him recover. Recover from being shot on duty a couple years ago.

Brenner had been the first Palm Beach Police Department officer shot there since 1951. Not a bad record for an agency.

The detective had started in the Tai Chi class and now was a regular in the karate and weapons classes. The two doctors taught more than one discipline at their eclectic school.

Dr. Ma and David closed the clinic and the school for the week. Their clinical manager Winnie, had been thrilled with a paid week off.

She couldn't wait for her grandchildren to arrive so they could head to Disney World in Orlando. David had gently teased her that she had never taken him to Disney World, and he was her most difficult child. Albeit, adopted. Unofficially.

Winnie had promised him a souvenir if he behaved himself for Dr. Ma. "I think I have gotten into enough trouble recently to warrant avoiding anything to upset Dr. Ma, Winnie," he had said.

"Mickey ears it is," Winnie had said. David made a face. "Minnie?" she had countered. "Ok, a t-shirt then." David had agreed to the last offer.

"I swear he will still attract everything within sight even if I dress him in a Mickey t-shirt," Winnie had confided to Dr. Ma when David walked away.

"Not a doubt," Ma said, grinning.

Now, the three Elementals were standing by Berenice's fountain in Ma's backyard. Ma touched the little stone statue's shoulder and she opened her blue eyes.

Dr. Ma dipped her hand the the fountain's water and they were suddenly standing in the Library. David realized Ma had taken his hand for the quick journey. He was not strong enough to go there on his own.

The journey had been quick to the Library, but he felt that uncomfortable tug whenever Dr. Ma brought him there. Something like being dragged through a tube of sandpaper was how he would describe it.

"Please imbed everything in your memory as we go David," Ma said in her instructional voice. "If anything ever happens to me, just carry me here and hold on to me. Berenice and Maia will get you safely into the Library if we have to leave the earthly plane.

Remember, I have to be touching you to get you through."

Allistair cleared his throat. "Unless I am available," he said matter of factly.

"Yes, of course," Ma agreed, "We are talking, in an emergency." She turned her attention back to David. "I had to get you into the Library before the fight with Circe, because it takes a lot of power to get you there.

"Maia had no problem getting you out, because your earth element was trying to leave that realm. Sort of like a cork under pressure."

David nodded. He was taking everything in. Ma had finally decided his abilities were at a level to teach him more about being an Elemental tiger. "Long learning curve," he thought, smiling to himself. "Only a thousand years."

"I heard that," Ma and Allistair said simultaneously.

"Your metabolism is much faster than mine or Allistair's, so we will have food for you, but a day or two there is a week here," Ma said to him. "You may feel very off when you come back. "I just don't know the total effect on you yet."

"I'm game," David said, smiling to reassure her. "Nothing to worry about."

"Says the uninitiated child," Allistair intoned.

"Just because time was invented after you were, there is no reason to be pissy," David said, smiling at him.

"No," Allistair corrected him. "That is Ma, I am much younger."

"Are you three going to stand there all day?" Berenice asked. She had been eyeing David carefully. Once they were all in the library, she could manifest in a form similar to theirs.

Nobody would need her on the outside end since they were all here. David was staring at her appreciatively. He had never seen her leave her stone stature and take a human guise. She was really beautiful.

"This is a serious visit, Berenice," Ma said, suppressing a smile. "You and Maia will have to restrain yourselves around the tiger, he is working!"

David flushed slightly. He knew both the ancient Otherworldly beings were overly interested in him.

"What the heck," he thought. "My track record with humans in piss poor and I haven't met a tiger who could match me since I first transformed."

Still looking at Berenice, he said aloud, "Maybe female Spirits would be better company."

Both Ma and Allistair frowned. Each wrapped a hand around one of his lean, muscular biceps and walked forward towards the center of the room.

All three heard the familiar squeak of Maia greeting them as she rushed forward. She stopped suddenly, looking at David before giggling like a school girl.

Berenice had followed them and was standing with her arms crossed over her chest, frowning.

"Am I going to have to put up with this the whole time we are here?" Allistair groaned, rolling his eyes.

"Oh stop it," Ma said, playfully slapping his arm. "You are just as big a school girl as they are where the tiger is concerned. You are just better at hiding it."

The Elemental snake smiled at her but didn't comment. Maia and Berenice regarding each other for a moment, each taking the other's measure before returning their attention to the three powerful Elementals standing together.

"If you will all just let him work now, I will leave him here a few days for you to play with when we are done," Ma offered the two ancient entities.

"Hey!," David said.

"Okay, on to the business at hand," Allistair said, eyeing Maia and Berenice. " I am not on vacation."

"Right! This place is, essentially, alive," Ma explained to David. There is nowhere to go per se. You stand here and ask for what you want and the dimension around you reconfigures to provide it."

"Avo's book, Circe's book, the compendium of Otherworldly beings on the earthly plane, furnishings and a glass of sherry," Allistair said, carefully enunciating each word. "Don't mumble," he said to David.

"The Library is rather old, and I fear, a bit hard of hearing."

"Stop," Ma rebuked him. "Not hard of hearing," she said to David, "Just meticulous in providing exactly what you ask for."

The requested books, tables, stools, chairs, couches and lamps arrived in record time. She gave Allistair a look as a table with a crystal glass and a decanter of sherry settled next to a particularly well padded velvet Louis IVX chair.

"Mine," Allistair said happily, as he settled into the padded chair and took a sip from the glass of ruby liquid.

Ma sighed and turned to David. "Just ask for food if you get hungry, child." Then she walked over to a couch with a large book on it and picked it up. In minutes, it looked like she was asleep, her eyes closed and the book open in her lap.

David knew the oddly covered book she held was Circe's. Ma was going to check up the the Sorceresses activities while she had been here, to make sure they hadn't missed a body, or worse.

Looking back at Maia and Berenice behind him, he started towards the reading table with a high stool. The ancient book there, open and waiting, must be Avo's Akashic record.

Ma's instruction before they left had been clear. "It is time you learned about your predecessor. Avo was a powerful Elemental and still is. He did many great things while he was here.

Reading his history will give you an advantage he never had. Learn from him."

David had agreed that this was an unprecedented offer. A bit intimidating, as each moment of a being's existence is recorded in their record. He was mostly concerned with Avo and Ma's personal relationship.

He wasn't sure how he would handle reading about their time together in such detail.

Allistair looked up at him. "Oh just sit down and get on with it," he said to David. "Be a big tiger. If you get uncomfortable reading any section, just skip through it. She mostly wants you to know about their battles and the foes they encountered.

Avo had impeccable strategies. You could use some of his cunning and stealth."

David smiled guiltily, remembering the slaughter he left behind in South Africa. "I am sure you are right about that," he said shyly. Allistair was a legendary Elemental, ancient and undefeated in battle.

David was sure he couldn't compare to either the snake or the dragon's skills. Yet.

Delicate laughter came from the back corner of the room. Berenice's voice was like tinkling bells and Maia's soft and harmonic, like wood wind instruments.

Not wanting to see them both still staring at him, David bent his head over Avo's book, randomly chose a section and began to read. In seconds he was lost in ancient history.

The two of them, Ama as Dr. Ma was called then and Avo, stood together on a high mountain crag. Icy winds whipped around them, Ma's hair billowing like a black cumulus cloud in the onslaught. Their foes waited below in the rift valley next to Lake Baikal, in Siberia.

Defeat was never out of the question in their job, but it wasn't what either Elemental thought about when entering into a battle. They had both been created for a purpose. Ama first, then Avo.

She had always been the element Air and Avo always the element Earth before their Adept had formed and shaped them into warriors. Two elements in balance to protect human kind on the earthly plane.

It was possible they had been something before, but if so, it was lost to memory too ancient to recall.

"Ready, my love?" Ama had said to Avo. They were communicating entirely in each other's mind. She in her Elemental dragon form and he is his Elemental tiger form would not have the ability to do so in any other way.

"Always," he had responded. "I am with you. I am always ready."

David could see the scene playing out as he read what looked like words on the page. He could feel the wind, their love for each other and the waiting fury of their opponents. It was almost like being there. He didn't like it at all. "Too much," he thought.

He had a sinking feeling this was where Avo died the last time on the earthly plane. Something had ripped him out of this existence and from away from Ma. That moment had necessitated his own creation.

Instead of reading further, David let himself sink into his own memories.

The massive female tiger stood over him, staring down at his battered and bloody body laying on the sand beneath her. They were in the flat sandy lands at the base of the Zagros Mountain range, on the southwestern border of what was Iran today.

In 900-1000 BCE, the area was considered ancient Persia, The Babylonian Empire, the building of Solomon's great temple and a flurry of activity on who would rule the greater parts of the expanding world of the ancient middle east was in full swing.

David had been born into a family of Greek descent. They had emigrated to the Zagros Mountain range and settled in for the long haul. Half the family of displaced high borns, demi gods all of them, took up residence in the mountain caves.

The other half settled in the valley below. Between the two settlements, they were unassailable.

After the death of his mother, Damon, as he was called then, was raised to be king of the mountain cave peoples. Powerful and possessing legendary skill in battle, he had been captured by his mother's sister, in a coup to bring both halves of the ancient Greek family under one rule.

Tortured and beaten for his lack of cooperation with her plans, Damon was thrown into the sandy flatlands by his aunt to die. He could remember it as if it was yesterday. Something poked at him while he waited to die from exposure.

Or by a predator. He was so badly injured, he didn't have the strength to try and save himself.

Opening his eyes to the massive head of the tiger looming over him, he lie there passively, throat and belly exposed to her sharp teeth. "Kill me," he said to her through a bloody mouth.

"Gladly, little one," the tiger replied in his thoughts. He was sure then he was delusional from pain and impending death. Tigers don't talk, especially in your thoughts. Accepting this, he answered her silently.

"Go on then, what are you waiting for? I cannot defend myself." he said, fading from consciousness a bit at a time. He felt something wet strike his cheek and looked up. It looked like a large tear had fallen onto him from one of her blue and yellow eyes. "Was the tiger, no, tigress crying?" he remembered thinking. "Maybe I am already dead."

Definitely a female from her voice. "Have I died and it just seems the same?" he asked her, his bloody mouth barely forming the words.

"No," her voice came to him in his head. "You are not dead, not yet. He waits for you, your creator," she said sadly.

"I must tell you that you will be reborn when I tear your throat out. Created to spend an eternity on earth helping humans. Keeping them safe from what others like you will become. Do you agree to this?"

"Better than what has happened so far," he said, fading further, his consciousness becoming spotty.

"But you will repeat this pattern when you are reborn each time, earth child," she said, her voice seeming to come from far away. "You will be born, suffer in the same way and live a lifetime doing what you were put there for. Each time she will find you."

Damon was losing track of what she was saying. All he could manage was, "Yes, agreed, kill me."

"David!" Ma said loudly, shaking him. David opened his eyes to see her next to him on the couch. Allistair stood next to her and Maia and Berenice hovered in the background.

"What?" he said sitting up.

"You were reading Avo's book and well, it isn't hard to get into a trance and re-experience your own origins," Ma said.

"I told you he wasn't ready," Allistair began.

"Quiet," Ma snapped at Allistair. "It's time, it will just take some adjustment."

"I'm fine," David said sitting up fully. "I was back in my own past, you were right. What did you two find out while I was, um, dreaming?" He was trying to get the attention off himself.

"Ladies?" Ma said, addressing Maia and Berenice. "Would you facilitate the transfer of dinner from Mort to us here? I know you two don't have to eat, but we still have human bodies to maintain.

"Dinner?" David asked, surprised. It had been early Saturday morning when they left the earthly realm.

"Yes," Ma said, watching him carefully as she spoke. "It is Sunday night at my house. You must be starved."

David just stared at her. "So, this is why you are so careful to have me watched here?"

"You could die here without knowing it," Ma agreed. "Time is irrelevant here, but your human body, different as it may be, is dependent on the cycles of time. Allistair and I have reptile metabolisms. We can go a few days, but you cannot."

The librarian and the fountain guardian re-appeared, loaded with food. Most for David, a light meal for Dr. Ma and a raw steak for Allistair. The snake saw David looking at the food and then at his decanter of sherry.

"I bring the cases here myself," Allistair said, answering his unspoken question. "That way the Library can provide it, just like the books and furniture.

David nodded and tucked into the large bowl of marinated raw veggies Mort had provided for him. Dr. Ma ate her meal and then began to tell the others what she had found out. Digestion first she always said about talking and eating.

"So," she began, "there *is* a leftover from Circe's visit. It walks in South Africa, near the Reserve. We will have to go back and retrieve it before it hurts someone."

"Is that how she poisoned me?" David asked. He was sitting back on the couch relaxed, with a full belly. The vision of the tiger who killed him had been replaced with the two spiritual entities on either side of him.

Actually, Berenice was much more solid than Maia, She looked as human and real as he and Ma did. She wasn't, but she looked it. They were both smiling at him.

"I saw a spear sticking out of your side," Ma said. "If I saw it, Circe saw it. If she saw it, she arranged it.

"David," Allistair said, finishing his last bloody bite of steak. "Didn't your girlfriend say something about that? Someone sticking the *tiger* who attacked the bad guys with a spear?"

At the mention of David's girlfriend, both entities on either side of David shifted uncomfortably. He could swear Maia was pouting. "She was *not* my girlfriend," he corrected. Both visibly perked up at the news.

"It's possible, but I don't remember that happening. I was, distracted," he said, looking embarrassed. He didn't like losing control. Blood and the heat of battle did that to him. Every time. He was hoping to gain some insight on that in Avo's records. Ma had mentioned her first tiger was cool and calculated under pressure.

"Well," Ma said. "The spear wielder turned in my observation from the book and he had our eyes."

"Not good," both David and Allistair said at the same time. Maia and Berenice nodded their agreement.

"Why don't you two go," Allistair offered. "I will stay here a bit and keep researching, um, more."

"Hmm," Ma said. "No way snake man. Leave your sherry and get the plane ready. We need to go and come back before our vacation is over. David and I have a practice to run."

"What about my firm?" Allistair countered. "I just got back from picking up the big guy here."

"Everyone knows you don't work at your firm, Allistair," David said laughing. "Besides, we can have some fun with all that time to kill in the air. Play board games, get to know each other better."

"Getting to know you better, tiger," Allistair said, arching one eyebrow and staring at him, "Wouldn't require a board game and would leave Ma alone to talk to the Captain and crew."

David got the gist immediately and flushed. "Some day snake," he said warningly. The entities on either side of him were trying not to laugh out loud.

Dr. Ma stood up. "Time to go, boys."

All three of them, four if you count Berenice, materialized in Dr. Ma's backyard. It was a velvety soft evening in South Florida. The heady smell of flowing plants mixed perfectly with the humid breeze from the Intracoastal Waterway.

"Thank you Berenice," Ma said at the beautiful Spirit again encased in stone to guard the Library entrance.

"How soon are we in the air?" Ma asked Allistair.

"Just pack now and we will all drive to my place in Miami," he replied. "We can leave from there as soon as the jet is ready and the flight plan filed."

They walked into Ma's elegant residence together. The dragon and the tiger went to pack. Allistair poured himself a glass of wine from Dr. Ma's well stocked bar and started making calls.

The last thing David heard as he walked into the guest bedroom Ma kept for his infrequent visits was Allistair saying, "Yes, I said tomorrow morning at the latest. Yes you idiot, South Africa. Again."

Epilogue

The old man, stood alone on the cliff, raw silk robes rippling in an unseen wind around his thin body,. The very cliff where she had so recently taken flight.

It was her first flight, one of many, but never one to return to him.

No, never. Ever. As it was supposed to be.

He had done his part. He made her and sent her off to do what was needed.

Very softly under his breath he said, "As long as time endures, and sentient beings remain on your Earth, good will prevail."

He was speaking to someone, unseen, but burned forever in his memories. Not her who just left. Someone else.

He took a final look in the direction he had last seen her in flight. "Good bye beautiful one," he said. The morning fog on the mountain, acrid from the decomposing earth, stung his eyes, making them tear.

"Or, was it her departure?" He sighed and refocused his powerful energies on the task ahead. "He must send her balance, a tiger, to go after her. To help her". This feat would be different, and exhausting.

Turning away, he retraced his route, slowly back down the mountain path.

About the Author

Lenore Maio is a Florida Licensed Acupuncture Physician residing in Palm Beach County Florida, the setting for the Dr. Ma Mystery series books.

Dr. Maio worked in emergency field medicine and law enforcement before attending graduate school and opening her Traditional Chinese Medical practice.Her speciality is sports medicine.

She lives with her spouse, two dogs and two cats along with an assortment of plants and outdoor critters to keep her company.

Dr. Maio is a long distance runner and cyclist as well as an avid gardener.

See more about the author, and other books she has written, at www.drmamysteries.com.

Coming soon…

"Twisting the Needle"

Book Three in the Dr. Ma Mystery Series:

Preview

Chapter One

The Spirit Winds she saw were never convenient. They didn't come and go in a timely manner. Their strength, length, and content were not predictable. But it was the job.

Riding with the Tuesday night cycling group that left from the base of the Lake Worth bridge was a guilty pleasure for Dr. Ma.

They started when Daylight Savings Time ensured they would have a couple hours of waning daylight to burn. They ended when the South Florida Winter, which was more about shorter days than colder weather, made it a full on dark ride.

Not that they didn't have headlights and taillights for their bikes. Again, this was more about it being the Winter season when the days were shorter. Combined with the elderly snow birds who would run you off the road and leave you lying there and well, it was interesting.

So, during late Spring, Summer and early Fall, she left David to handle classes at the Dojo and rode with the small group of fast, some elite, cyclists that practically flew along. One tightly behind the other, they rode east over the bridge and then north on A1A.

The fact that this particular Spirit Wind chose to catch her on her bike just after the ride wasn't endearing its story to Dr. Ma. She would have to pull over and let it come.

She was heading into downtown West Palm Beach with night falling. Not the best place to stop all alone, either.

Dr. Ma was not afraid of anything on the current earthly plane but, she had healthy respect for some. Like criminals with guns. If she saw them first, there was no contest. She won.

Dealing with a Spirit Wind however, could make her a bit vulnerable, slow to respond. David would come to her and help her in Spirit form only. She also couldn't just walk into a crowded restaurant or coffee shop. The slight fugue state she would enter could be enough to have them call an ambulance or law enforcement to help her.

She slowed her bike coming west over the Okeechobee Bridge and turned north on Flagler Drive. Pulling off the road and stepping onto the broad concrete walkway that bordered the Intracoastal Waterway, she guided her bike next to her.

She saw one of the public benches that dotted the walkway, and made her way towards it.

"Dr. Ma?" she heard her name called. Turning her head, she saw her friend Detective Jeremy Brenner waving at her out of his car window.

"Oh no," she groaned inwardly. "This just got better and better." She could hear the howling of the Spirit Wind closer now. The last thing she wanted was to have Jeremy there when it arrived.

Brenner quickly parked his POV (personal off-duty vehicle) in one of the parallel spaces next to the walkway and hopped out. He had been wanting to speak with Ma about a case that NYPD had asked him to consult on yesterday.

He followed her to the bench where she leant her bike along the waist high concrete abutment to the Intracoastal Waterway.

Ma could feel the Wind now, she could smell the first batch of scents related to the crime. She had no choice but to involve Jeremy. "Please sit down on the bench with me," she said firmly, hurrying over to the bench.

Jeremy Brenner stopped mid sentence and looked at her. He had just started to tell her about his case referral. "Are you alright?" were his first words.

The cop was all business in moments when a difficult situation presented itself. He knew immediately that things weren't right.

"Please just go with what is about to happen Jeremy," Ma said, in anything but a pleading tone of voice. She was his martial arts teacher as well as his physician. She was used to giving him direction.

"I need you to sit with me and not say or do anything until I am ready. Don't let anything interrupt me. I won't be fully able to respond to any interruption or threat in a few minutes. I will explain later."

Brenner didn't waste time with small talk. Whatever was about to happen didn't matter as much as handling it well. He almost pulled her down onto the bench with him. Anyone passing might have though they were lovers about to cuddle in the dark.

Ma turned to face him and wrapped her arms around his waist to steady herself. She rested her head on his shoulder in the crook of his neck. Then, she went very still.

Jeremy could smell her hair. Her nearness and the intimacy of her embrace was creeping through his tough professional exterior. Dr. Ma was a beautiful woman. He had admired her for years.

Locked in a gentle, almost loving embrace, his throat felt tight and he fought any response his body may consider to her proximity. She sighed softly into his neck and he bit his lip to stay focused.

Dr. Ma may have seemed quiet and peaceful on the outside, but the raging storm within was causing her a problem. She had called out to David when she first stopped her bike. Still at the dojo, several students around, David tried to make some quick excuses and escape into the attached Traditional Chinese Medical Clinic. Sosam Li, one of their student teachers, dogged David's steps.

Entering the back door of the clinic, it was almost too late. David, hearing the screaming Wind, saw Ma resting in Jeremy Brenner's arms on a bench by the Intracoastal Waterway.

He pushed his surprised reaction at their circumstances away to try and focus on containing the Wind for her.

She was in the middle of the maelstrom, being buffeted by the strangely strong Wind. She was calling his name.

David felt himself pulled into the Spirit vision with her and dropped suddenly to his knees in the hallway. Sosa Li, still right behind him, ran the few steps between them and knelt beside his beloved instructor.

"Sifu!" he shouted, wrapping his arms around David's waist and trying to lift him up. The powerful man felt like he weighed a thousand pounds. "What the hell?" Li thought to himself.

David knew he had to grapple the Wind for Ma or risk both of them lost in the melee until it was over. Lost and perhaps missing important information about a murder they could not recover when it was gone.

He gave a superhuman effort to press the energy of the Wind between his powerful hands. Li watched a brighter patch of light than the surrounding hallway, bloom between David's hands.

He had seen great masters manipulate Qi before. From training with David and Dr. Ma for many years, he knew they were both the greatest of all the masters he had ever seen.

David's eyes were closed while he knelt in the hallway, pressing the ball of Qi between his hands, palm facing together, the ball rolling North and South, compressing the images whirling around Dr. Ma in the vision.

Holding them still.

On her end, Ma finally started to make sense of the images and sensations tearing at her in a cyclone of activity. She could see David kneeling in the hallway of their clinic, Sosam Li next to him, watching the ball of Qi in David's hands. "Oh no," Ma thought briefly, "that will have to be dealt with."

Immersing herself in the Spirit Wind, Ma let every detail available of the crime absorb into her very essence. All she had to do was be a sponge and the information would attach itself. Her inner vision was fully open. Safe in Jeremy's arms, she could let go and let it saturate her.

This one was powerful. She could see David trembling slightly with the effort to contain it. The only Wind that powerful would be that of an Adept. Ma knew the identity of the Spirit would be revealed fully when they were done. She had absorbed enough. She nodded slightly to David.

Jeremy felt her stir slightly in his arms. It had been at least 5 or more minutes since Ma had embraced him and gone still. He couldn't see his watch in the dark.

He had wrapped his arms around her to make them look more natural sitting together. His eyes watched the darkness like any good cop. Watching for any threat to come their way.

David spun the ball of Qi to an East and West position and set it free. Li watched the glow fade from between David's hands as he slumped forward, groaning.

"I was NOT expecting THAT," David mumbled to himself. It had been very strong, that Wind. Containing them when they first arrived was not as difficult as wrestling them into submission when they were in full rampage mode.

He vaguely wondered who died? "Surely a powerful Adept," he thought.

Remembering suddenly that Li was kneeling next to him, holding him up, David stood unsteadily and pulled his student up with him. They ended up standing very close in the hallway.

Li closed the distance and put his arms around him as if still holding him up. "Sifu, what happened?" Li asked.

David could sense the deep attraction Li felt for him and gently put his hands on his student's arms and pulling back out of his embrace. Li's face fell suddenly.

"Li," David said softly, face to face with the younger man. "I'm fine, thank you so much for helping me."

Li looked up, quickly hiding his disappointment that David had pulled away. Li had been gay all his life and both his instructors knew about him. It didn't matter to them in the least. Except for his attraction to David.

The Mugen Dojo had an iron clad no fraternization between students and teachers code. Period. As it should be.

Li understood, but had never given up hope. He knew many gay men in Palm Beach who were interested in David. While it seemed the sexy martial arts teacher and acupuncture physician was open and friendly with everyone who flirted with him, he didn't have a girlfriend or boyfriend.

Li thought it was just odd. Hot guy, no action. Odd.

"I think my blood sugar was low,"David said in explanation. Li was skeptical as best. "I was going to grab some snacks here, but, what about me treating you to a late dinner for helping me?" he asked Li.

Sosam Li thought his birthday had just come early. He may never get his instructor into bed in this lifetime but, a couple of hours talking and eating together was more than he usually managed with the shy, gorgeous man.

David watched Li's expression brighten. He grabbed a couple of his raw nut bars from the refrigerator in his office and handed Li one. "Let me take a quick shower," he said to Li. "How about you?" he offered.

Li's heart skipped a whole beat. "We have two in the back." His heart rate returning to normal, Li declined. He wasn't sure taking his clothes off around David was a wise decision and, he didn't have a change of clothes anyway.

Meanwhile, by the darkened waterfront, Dr. Ma had recovered herself and disentangled from her embrace with Jeremy. The velvety evening had deepened around them. Less than savory characters were appearing here and there.

"Let's put your bike in my POV and grab some coffee,"Jeremy said to Ma, trying to shake off the intimacy of their recent embrace. "Are you alright? Do I have to take you to a walk in clinic first or something?"

"No," she said. "I see things Jeremy, that is how I help you with your cases. Sometimes I get a vision and it incapacitates me for a few minutes."

"Oh," Brenner said, nonplussed. What she said was a surprise but it sounded completely truthful and even plausible. He was seen things like that on TV. He just didn't know he would participate in one with Dr. Ma. "So, coffee still sounds good?"

"Great!" Ma said. The particular road bike she was riding tonight broke down easily and would slip into Jeremy's trunk without an issue. "Why did you flag me down?" she asked him.

"I have a case I wanted to consult with you about from," he began before she interrupted him.

"NYPD?" she asked.

Brenner's mouth hung open. "How in the hell does she do that," he thought. Aloud he just stammered, "Yes."

"I think I may know who your killer is," Ma answered.

Their conversation was interrupted by the sudden appearance of a Water Sprite on the concrete barrier wall next to the walkway.

The wall ran the length of the Intracoastal Waterway through West Palm Beach and Lake Worth. It changed in height and decoration as it changed the neighborhoods it protected from rising water.

"Ma-sama," the little creature said in its tinny, metal on metal voice.

"What the f-ck?" Jeremy Brenner said, looking at the little creature.

Too late Dr. Ma realized he was seeing what she was seeing. Too late the Water Sprite realized the human detective could see him as clearly as Dr. Ma. Ma looked down and saw Jeremy's hand on her arm. He was probably going to take her bike from her to put in his trunk.

Brenner was fast. He slipped his arm around Dr. Ma, pulling her behind him in a protective manner. As one arm pulled her back, the other pulled his firearm from its shoulder holster. "Nicely done," Ma couldn't help thinking.

The Otherworldly creature froze, too frightened to move. Dr. Ma moved. She took a step forward with her right foot from behind him, placing her hip in front of his and shot her right hand across his body, wrapping her hand around the slide of the automatic weapon by reaching under his outstretched arm.

Too fast to register, she had stripped the firearm from his hand without it firing. The Water Sprite disappeared with a soft splash and Brenner looked at her in disbelief. "What?" was all he got out.

Dr. Ma went with it. "Have you been drinking?" she asked Jeremy in rebuke. "What on earth are you doing?" She had stepped sideways after relieving him of his gun. She still held her bike in one hand and his Glock .45 caliber semi automatic hand gun in the other.

Brenner reached for the firearm only to have one of Dr. Ma's feet crack into his wrist in a precise strike. His hand went numb.

He was recovering enough to realize this was a no win situation. Her skills were beyond him and he was still trying to process why he had drawn his gun in the first place.

He was staring hard at the place he had seen the odd looking, well he didn't have a name for it, but it was like something out of a movie.

Maybe two feet tall at tops, it glowed a soft green with silvery eyes and the general appearance of one of those Troll Dolls from the 60's. His mother had one in her bedroom from her childhood.

 He blinked hard and shook his head. Then he walked closer to the retaining wall and looked over it for a moment. It had spoken, the Troll Doll looking creature. Some weird sounding language like rubbing two tin cans together.

Looking back at her, he stammered, "Didn't you see it?"

"See what?" Dr. Ma said, her voice neutral. She felt terrible doing this to him. She just didn't know what else to say. Her mind was racing. Jeremy had never seen anything Otherworldly before in her or David's presence.

"Did him holding her during the arrival of the Spirit Wind change something?" she thought.

"I must be working too many hours," he said, rubbing his hands over his face. He looked up and held his hand out authoritatively. "Please return my firearm, I am not a danger to anyone, I swear."

She frowned at him and walked closer, looking at him carefully. Handing him his firearm grip first, muzzle pointing down, she said, "I have never seen you do anything like that. You need to get some sleep or maybe see a doctor."

"Yes," he said vaguely. "Seriously, you saw nothing?"

"No," she said firmly. Changing the subject and hoping to return things to a semblance of normalcy, she said, "I do have to thank you again for being here for me."

He helped her put her bike and its now separate font wheel away. She closed his trunk and walked around the front passenger seat. Slipping into his front seat she said, "Starbucks?"

Jeremy shook his head affirmatively and got into the drivers side. Starting the engine, he looked over at her and asked, "I suppose you plan on telling me more about what happened back there with you on the bench? Like what you saw and how often this kind of thing happens?"

"Of course not, Jeremy," Ma answered laughing. "Since when do I tell you everything?"

"Never," he responded quickly. He smiled at her. "I am just glad to have been there when you needed me. If you ever decide to tell me fine. If not, no worries. I really apologize for freaking out on you and drawing my gun. Our secret?"

Ma smiled at Jeremy with real affection. She had become attached to him from working their cases together, Still, there were many things Jeremy would never know about her and David. Much he could never understand.

"I am glad you were there too. Nothing to worry about as far as me telling anyone that you are officially seeing things. You can describe your new imaginary friend to me. Coffee?"

In their Traditional Chinese Medicine clinic, David toweled off, glad that Li had turned down his offer of a shower and was currently sitting in the beautiful waiting area of the clinic. Golds and reds were the predominant colors along with every conceivable shade of green. The overall effect was calming but warm.

"What was I thinking?" he chided himself. He knew Li was gay and very attracted to him. "A shower? In the clinic, alone?" David amazed himself at times.

Dressing in a pair of faded jeans and a polo shirt, David joined Sosam Li in the clinic waiting area. "Ready? Thai Express in Lantana, my treat?" he said. He knew it was one of Li's favorite places.

Sosam Li looked at his teacher standing there in his soft, faded jeans and shirt. "He is so incredibly handsome," Li thought.

Tousled blond hair pulled back in a loose pony tail, only towel dry. Gorgeous blue eyes and sharp angels to his face set off a sensuous mouth. His 6'5" frame was an anatomical study of muscle covered in golden tanned skin.
Li sighed.

"At least I can show off being with him," he thought. Thai Express had a large gay male clientele. David was a very attentive 'date,' hanging on your every word when he was with you. Always the perfect, sexy gentleman. "They will all be so jealous," he thought.

"Let's do it," Li said, hoping it sounded neutral enough. He waved his keys. "I suppose I am driving?"

Everyone knew David didn't drive. Not everybody knew that it was because he was color blind. Every good tiger, Elemental or not, was pretty color blind.

At least enough to not pass a driving test. David never seemed to have a lack of rides if needed. Li knew he ran most places or walked.

The two of them left out the back door, carefully locking up and checking the alarm. Then they set the alarm and locked up in the dojo next door.

Getting into Li's car, David figured he would see Dr. Ma in the morning. They had a lot to discuss after her vision tonight. Another murder, surely.

Enjoy your preview? Pre-order it now on Amazon Kindle! www.amazon.com

For further updates go to www.drmamysteries,com. Get on the author's mailing list, read her blog, learn about new titles coming out!

Thank you for being a fan!

www.ingramcontent.com/pod-product-compliance
Lightning Source LLC
Chambersburg PA
CBHW062020170626
46813CB00001B/228